Here it was... What she'd come here for.

All Serena needed was the courage to go through with it.

Taking one slow step after another, she walked toward Jack and kept her gaze fixed to his every movement. She saw the flare of heat, the glint of desire, and it kindled the burning embers inside her into a bonfire ready to rage. "I don't want to go out," she whispered.

"What do you want?" he asked, catching her hand with his and holding her palm to his chest.

Serena tipped her head back until she was looking directly into his eyes. "You, Jack. I want *you*."

Ways to Win an Ex by Maureen Child is part of the Dynasties: The Carey Center series.

DYNASTIES

The Carey Center is a performance hall like no other, and the Carey family will fight, forgive and find love as they make it the star of the California coast.

Amanda, Serena, Bennett and Justin—don't miss a single Carey family story!

Dear Reader,

I'm having so much fun with the Carey family. Serena Carey is especially fun for me because her hero, Jack Colton, has popped back into her life after being gone for seven years.

But this time, Serena has her daughter, Alli, to think about, and Jack's not sure he's father material.

Serena's stronger than she used to be and meeting Jack again tests that strength in every possible way. As she carves out a life for herself within the Carey family, Jack is a constant, *tempting* reminder that life is about more than just work.

I really hope you enjoy the second book in the Carey Center series. Please stop by my Facebook page and let me know what you think!

Until next time, happy reading!

Maureen

MAUREEN CHILD

WAYS TO WIN AN EX

HARLEQUIN

DESIRE

Recycling programs
for this product may
not exist in your area.

ISBN-13: 978-1-335-73523-2

Ways to Win an Ex

Copyright © 2021 by Maureen Child

Harlequin Enterprises ULC
22 Adelaide St. West, 40th Floor
Toronto, Ontario M5H 4E3, Canada
www.Harlequin.com

Printed in U.S.A.

Maureen Child writes for the Harlequin Desire line and can't imagine a better job. A seven-time finalist for the prestigious Romance Writers of America RITA® Award, Maureen is the author of more than one hundred romance novels. Her books regularly appear on bestseller lists and have won several awards, including a Prism Award, a National Readers' Choice Award, a Colorado Romance Writers Award of Excellence and a Golden Quill Award. She is a native Californian but has recently moved to the mountains of Utah.

Books by Maureen Child

Harlequin Desire

Tempt Me in Vegas
Bombshell for the Boss
Red Hot Rancher
Jet Set Confessions
Temptation at Christmas
Six Nights of Seduction

Dynasties: The Carey Center

The Ex Upstairs
Ways to Win an Ex

Visit her Author Profile page at Harlequin.com, or maureenchild.com, for more titles.

You can also find Maureen Child on Facebook, along with other Harlequin Desire authors, at Facebook.com/harlequindesireauthors!

To Patti and Bill Hambleton for so many reasons. You were there in the darkness and kept a light burning for me. You held me together when I thought that would be impossible. You loved him, too, and you help me smile at the memories.

I'm so grateful for you both. And I love you.

One

"This is the way we've always done things, Serena."

Her mother, Candace, stood in Serena Carey's office and looked down at her. "You're making so many changes, I just don't know how it can all work out. Heaven knows, I don't want to interfere…"

But you're going to, Serena thought. Every year, the Carey Center hosted a fundraiser for their charitable organization, For the Kids. It was the biggest event of the year and donors came from far and wide to be part of it.

And until *this* year, Candace Carey had been in charge. But she'd handed over the reins—in theory—

to Serena six months ago. Now it seemed the older woman was having a few second thoughts.

"Mom," Serena said patiently, "everything is handled. You have to trust me on this."

Candace linked her fingers together at the waist and started pacing in slow, elegant steps. Everything Candace did was elegant, Serena told herself, not without a little envy. Then her mother stopped, turned to look at her and bit her lip for a moment before speaking again. "Of course I trust you, Serena. But when we talked about this six months ago, you didn't mention making so many changes. Music. Food. Flowers. Everything is changing and I just don't know if it's the right thing to do." She actually wrung her hands a bit, and that was so unlike the unflappable Candace that Serena felt a little guilty for throwing so many changes at her mother all at once.

"Change isn't always a bad thing, Mom," Serena pointed out. "For example, the cinnamon highlights in your hair are fabulous."

Candace perked up, smoothed one hand over her short, elegant cut. "You're trying to smooth me out, I can tell. And you're very good at it. But, honey, the gala is the biggest event of the year. The children are counting on the money we collect from our donors…"

Serena stood up, came around her desk and took both of her mom's hands in hers. "Do you really think if the flowers are different people won't donate to the charity?"

"There's something to be said for tradition, you know," her mother countered without answering the question. "For example, we've always used the Swing Masters for the music and—"

"Mom…" Serena had known going in that there would be some pushback when she wanted to make changes. Which was the reason, she told herself, she hadn't mentioned those changes six months ago. Remembering that her mother was the one who had started this charity and built it into a real giant, Serena took a breath, then said gently, "The Swing Masters are in their seventies now."

"What does that have to do with anything?"

Age was tricky since her parents were quickly closing in on seventy themselves. But she persisted. "Mom, they're retired. They only get together again now to play for the fundraiser."

"Exactly."

Serena squeezed her mom's hands, then let her go. "The new band can play the old standards, as well as more modern music. I think our donors will enjoy it."

"I don't know…"

Serena had already talked to Leo Banks, the lead guitarist in the Swing Masters, and had been assured that they were perfectly happy to stay retired. So she just hugged her mom and smiled. "Trust me."

"I do, but so many changes all at once…" Candace shook her head and her short chestnut hair swung gracefully at her jaw. And the cinnamon highlights really did look spectacular. "You've hired a roaming photographer, as well?"

"Yes, and you're going to love it." Serena tamped down her impatience. She'd only been back working at the Carey Center for a couple of years, so she was going to have to earn her family's respect and confidence.

Growing up, she'd never been interested in having a career. Actually, she'd never had a plan for her life at all like her siblings always seemed to—well, except for Justin, of course. All she'd really wanted was to find love and have a family of her own. Well, that hadn't worked out so well, had it? Now her marriage was over and she was trying to discover what exactly she wanted for her life. And Serena was slowly learning how to speak up—and stand up—for herself. All her life, Serena had been willing to go with the flow. She hadn't made waves because nothing had really meant enough to her to fight for it.

Serena was teaching herself how to take a stand, because now building a life for herself and her daughter was everything. Working for the family was safe, but carving out her own space in the business was hard. She loved her family, but they weren't used to seeing her give her opinions and, she realized, that was her own fault because she'd always been the easygoing one. The peacemaker. And though she still preferred serenity, that was something she'd never really experience with the Careys.

Even the thought of it made her chuckle internally. Her family would never be called tranquil. And she wouldn't change them for anything. What she had to do was navigate the sometimes churning waters. And she was learning how to do that.

Serena was still too hesitant about speaking her mind, but she was getting better. Right now, she was finding her feet. Figuring out her path. And nobody had ever promised her it would be easy.

"It'll be fun, Mom. The photographer's got some great ideas and a fantastic reputation. People are going to love it." At least she hoped so. Her own future with the family business was riding on the success of the annual fundraiser. Yes, she'd made changes because, frankly, the bash had become a little staid. A little too ordinary. Nothing ever changed, and though people still attended, and they were still able to raise huge amounts of money for the charity, Serena thought the event itself should be more…fun.

Serena had gone over all her ideas with her sister, Amanda, and she'd loved them, too. So Serena wasn't really *worried*. Just…concerned. A little. And her mom's doubts weren't helping anything.

"The photographer is going to wander through the crowd, taking random shots, and then we'll flash the images onto two screens at opposite ends of the ballroom." Serena had contracted with the top photographer in Orange County, California, and trusted the woman would deliver on everything she had promised.

Candace bit her bottom lip.

Serena continued, and the more she talked about it, the better she felt. "Everyone at the gala will get a kick out of seeing themselves and their friends and families up on the big screens. And if anyone wants to buy prints, they can deal with the photographer directly. After the gala, we're going to post the images on our website, as a direct advertisement about what a great time everyone had— which will only increase donations *next* year."

Candace tipped her head to one side, studied her daughter for a long moment or two, then said, "You've done a lot of thinking about this. About all of it."

Yes, she had. Life might not have turned out exactly the way Serena had hoped it would, but she'd discovered that she was good at working with people. She liked pulling plans together and finding a way to make everything mesh. The gala was going to be her first big success—hopefully—and it was nice to have her mother notice.

"I have. Mom, you turned the gala over to me, and I promise I'm not going to let you down. It's going to be great." *Please*, let it be great. If the whole thing flopped, she'd never hear the end of it from the family. Already, her older brother, Bennett, was also questioning every change.

And her mother… Well, Candace had been in charge of the program for decades and had only handed over the reins because she'd believed her husband when he promised to retire. But since Martin was having a hard time letting go, Candace was fighting to regain control. And Serena was going to stand her ground.

This was new for her and she was sure a psychiatrist would have a field day with her motivations. But the truth was, she'd stood by when the man she loved broke her heart. And, God, she didn't even want to remember that she'd silently done nothing while he walked away from her.

Worse, though, was that Serena had allowed that suffocating pain to blind her to the faults of the man she'd married. And she hated knowing that it had taken forever for her to stand up for herself with Robert. But she finally had. She'd gotten a divorce and full custody of Alli and learned that she didn't *have* to be a doormat.

She still wasn't sure if the Carey Corporation

was what she wanted to do for the rest of her life, but, damn it, she was here now. And she was going to make her mark and let everyone know that Serena Carey was no longer a pushover. And they had no one to blame but themselves. Because for some reason, since she'd entered the family business, she'd begun picking up some of the Carey family's ingrained competitive streak. Good thing? Bad thing? Who knew?

"I do have some ideas on the catering…"

Serena gave her mom's hand a quick squeeze and lied. Yes, she felt a little guilty, but she needed a break. "You know, so do I, and I've got a meeting with Margot Davis to go over the menu again in a few minutes."

"Oh, good. I'm happy to help with that," Candace said.

"But I think Amanda wanted to talk to you this morning about one of the acts for the Summer Sensation program." She should probably feel guilty for tossing her younger sister under the bus, but she didn't. It was just a small lie. A necessary one, and Serena would no doubt pay for it once she saw her sister.

"Oh." Candace nodded, smiled and said, "Then I'll go see your sister. But I would like to go over the menu for the fundraiser with you, Serena. After lunch?"

Smothering a sigh, she said, "Sure, Mom."

With her mother gone, Serena walked around her desk and dropped into the cream-colored leather chair. Swiveling around, she stared out the window at the greenbelt below the building that wound through the neighboring chrome-and-glass office buildings like a thick ribbon. In the distance, she could see the 405 Freeway and, well beyond that, a blue smudge that was the Pacific Ocean. And right about now, she wished she were standing on the shore, with the wind sliding through her hair and no sound but the pounding of the waves onto the sand.

"But since I'm not…" Serena turned around, picked up the phone and called Margot. "Hi," she said when the caterer answered. "Any chance you could come in now and meet about the menu? I know we were set for this afternoon, but I'd like to get it all ironed out before the rest of the family sees it."

"Absolutely." Margot Davis was as eager for the success of the fundraiser as Serena was. The annual gala at the Carey Center would be the biggest showcase the chef had ever had for her work and it could set her reputation for the future. "I can be there in half an hour."

"Terrific. See you then." When she hung up, Serena reassured herself that everything was working as it should. She had a great band lined up, a terrific new caterer that she'd found through a comprehensive search, a florist who was going to decorate the ballroom with tasteful, beautiful displays. She was in complete control. Nothing was going to go wrong.

Her assistant buzzed in. "What is it, Kelly?"

"There's a Jack Colton here to see you."

And just like that, a perfectly good day turned to crap.

She'd jinxed herself, of course, by thinking about how great things were going. That would teach her.

Scowling at the phone, she said, "Tell him I went to Tahiti."

With a little more warning, it was exactly what she would have done, rather than face Jack again.

The man she'd once loved and hoped to marry. The man she'd watched walk away from her. The man who was still appearing in her dreams, ensuring that she woke up hot and aching and furious with herself that even in her sleep Jack could turn her inside out. Her heartbeat sped up and she took a deep breath, trying to calm herself. It didn't help. Just knowing he was right outside her door made her…shaky.

With any luck, he'd simply go away.

An instant later, her office door opened and there he stood. Serena wasn't surprised. As she remembered it, nothing could stop Jack when he was determined to do something. That fact was both irritating and admirable. At the moment, she was going with irritation.

And, damn it, captivated.

She couldn't take her eyes off him. Was he even taller than he used to be? He stood well over six feet, with too long black hair that curled over the collar of his white shirt, and eyes as deep and dark as a sapphire. He gave her a half smile, closed her office door, then swept the edges of his black suit jacket back to tuck his hands into his slacks pockets. "Tahiti's changed. But you haven't. As gorgeous as ever, Serena."

She refused to be charmed.

"Really?" she asked with a short laugh. "I haven't seen you in seven years and the first thing you say is some lame compliment?"

"Not lame at all," he countered. "You're still beautiful."

"And you're still fast with meaningless flattery." She smiled and shook her head. "I'm not a simpleton, Jack. That's not going to get you very far."

He shrugged that off with another half smile that made her gullible heart do a quick flip. "It's not flattery if it's true."

Now she was annoyed with herself. Seven years since she'd seen him and one look at him had her pulse pounding in spite of the way he'd ended things between them. Back then, Serena had been so... timid. She hadn't said a word when he walked away from her. Hadn't let him know that he'd ripped her heart out when he left. She hadn't been capable of standing up for herself then. But she'd changed. She wasn't the Serena he remembered. And just because her body was overreacting, it didn't mean she was going to do anything about it. "Go away, Jack."

"But I just got here."

Serena stood up because she wasn't going to stay seated while he stood as tall as a giant. Why wasn't he covered in boils or pimples? Why did he have to look so *good*? "What do you want, Jack?"

"Well, thanks for asking." He pulled his hands from his pockets and strolled across the room, like a man with nothing but time. He glanced around and she followed his gaze, seeing her office as he must be seeing it.

Pale rose walls, with framed photographs of the family dotting one wall. There was a plump, comfortable sofa, two matching armchairs and, on the opposite wall from her desk, a flat-screen TV. A library table held a small fridge and a single-cup coffee maker. The floors were polished oak, dotted with area rugs in faded jewel-toned colors.

"Your office is very like you," he pointed out, and she hated that he knew her well enough to notice. Not that she'd admit that.

"Think you know me, do you?"

"Always have," he said, and his voice seemed to rumble along her spine, sending a shiver she refused to acknowledge right down to her bones. He studied her for a long moment before adding, "Though there's something…different about you, too."

She choked out a short laugh of derision. "Wow, imagine that. I've changed in seven years. Let's see. Marriage. Having a child. Divorce. Joining the family company. Yeah," she said, nodding thoughtfully. "I suppose I am different."

"Touché," he said and bowed his head briefly in acknowledgment.

Steadying herself, Serena simply said, "I don't have time for this, Jack. Why are you here?"

"Right to business," he countered. "That's different, too. I don't remember you being interested in the Carey company."

She hadn't been. Then. "Like I said. Changes."

"Okay then, business. For starters, I want to buy a table at the fundraiser."

Well, that was a surprise. She hadn't seen Jack in years. Not since the night she'd confessed her love for him. He'd left the country the following day to *concentrate on the Colton Group hotel chain. Or to run and hide*, she mentally corrected.

After she'd picked up her shattered heart and taped it back together again, Serena remembered wondering if she was the only woman who'd had a man actually leave the *country* to get away from her.

"Why would you want to do that?" she asked.

"Supporting children in need? Sounds like a good cause to me."

"And you're all about altruism?"

One corner of his mouth tipped up. "Are you this hard on all of your donors?"

Serena locked her fingers together in front of her. "No, you're special."

His lips twitched and she nearly smiled.

"You've been gone for seven years, Jack. How do you even know about the fundraiser?"

"Please. The Carey gala has been one of the biggest events of the year for more than thirty years."

True.

"And," he added, "Bennett told me it was still on."

Serena smiled wryly. "Of course he did."

Jack laughed and walked closer. "I came in today to see him, let him know I was moving back to the States permanently."

Wary now, she watched him. "You are?"

"Yeah." He nodded, keeping his gaze fixed on hers. "I'll still have to travel to Europe for business, but this will be home."

Great. When Jack moved to London seven years ago, it actually helped Serena get over him. She knew he was far from California and she wouldn't be bumping into him all the time, so she could push him out of her mind and heart and keep him there. Then she'd met and married Robert and *mostly* stopped thinking about Jack at all.

Now he was moving back. And since he and Bennett were friends, that meant she'd probably be seeing a lot of Jack. Not that Serena was worried about being around him. She wasn't. Not at all. She simply didn't like to be reminded of mistakes, and having Jack around would be nothing but a constant reminder.

"So," he continued, snapping her out of her thoughts, "I think fifty thousand for a table at your gala is a good way to announce it."

Buying an entire table was certainly generous, but Serena wasn't so willing to make things easy on him. How like Jack Colton to stroll in and expect everything to roll his way. Well, not this time. "That is the usual price for a full table, Jack, but it's late. The gala is in just a couple weeks."

His eyes narrowed on her and Serena almost smiled. Almost.

"So the price of a table's gone up?"

She did smile then. She was about to find out how badly he wanted to make a statement at the gala. "Seventy-five thousand should do it."

Silence strung out between them as he watched her for a second or two before nodding. "All right, Serena. You make a fair point. I did come in late. And it is for a good cause, right?"

"Absolutely." And she had to admit, she was

surprised. He hadn't even blinked when she raised the price on him. So did that mean he wanted to impress her? Was that part of the plan? Or was he simply so eager to get back into the life he'd walked away from that price was no object?

He walked closer to her desk and looked down at her. "Then put the Colton Group down for a table and I'll have my assistant wire you the money this afternoon."

Serena sat back in her chair and slowly, casually crossed her legs. "As soon as we've received the money, I'll reserve your table."

Jack laughed shortly. "No trust for an old friend?"

"Is that what we are?" Serena met his gaze and thought of all the things she could say. That they were never friends. That the connection between them had been so blistering hot, it was like trying to live on the surface of the sun. That they'd been lovers within hours of meeting and they hadn't parted until she'd whispered those three words designed to separate the men from the boys. That he'd broken all trust between them when he'd shattered her heart and left her standing alone in the rubble. She could have said all of that and more, but she didn't say any of it. "Friends?"

He shrugged. "If you want to be, sure."

"I have enough friends."

"Funny," he said. "Me, too." Another step closer. "So where does that leave us?"

Her heart pounded in her ears. Her blood rushed through her veins. Breathing was suddenly an effort, and still she looked into his eyes and said simply, "Nowhere, Jack. Exactly nowhere."

He tucked his hands into his pants pockets and strolled leisurely around the room. His gaze swept the framed photos and Serena felt as if he were examining her life. Her world. She didn't like it.

"Not true, Serena," he finally said and turned to face her. "We may not be friends, but for the moment, we will be working together."

She had a bad feeling about this. "What are you talking about?"

"Like I said, I was talking to Bennett about an idea I had that could help both of us and create some real buzz around the donations."

"Buzz?" Serena laughed shortly and pushed her butterscotch-blond hair back from her face. "The Carey Center *is* buzz. So thanks, but the Careys have been handling our own parties and events for a long time. I really don't think we need any new *ideas* from you." Though, apparently, her older brother thought so.

Did everyone in her family think she was incapable of running the gala and making it a success? Now Bennett was sticking his nose in and encouraging Jack to do the same?

His gaze locked with hers. "Don't dismiss it so quickly, Serena. You could at least hear the idea before shooting it down. What I'm proposing will get people talking. It will bring in even more money than usual to the fundraiser."

Okay, she could admit, at least to herself, that she was curious. Because if the gala raised more money than ever before while *she* was in charge, well, the family would have to notice, wouldn't they? She could finally put her own stamp on one corner of the Carey Corporation. And, frankly, it would convince the family—and maybe even herself—that she was capable of whatever she put her mind to. But to do that, she'd have to work with Jack Colton.

Nope. She'd find another way to show the family what she could do.

"Well," she said, moving out from behind her desk, "while it's fascinating that you and Bennett want to *help*, it's not necessary, thanks."

He folded his arms across his wide chest and braced his feet apart as if readying for a battle. Well, if he wanted one, she'd be happy to provide it.

"Bennett likes my idea," he said pointedly. "A lot."

She lifted her chin. "Bennett's not in charge."

One eyebrow arched. "You should tell him that."

"Oh, I will," she promised, already planning what she would say to her older brother.

"Great." He let his arms drop to his sides, then idly tucked his hands into his pockets again. "But first I'll tell you about the idea and then you'll know what you're arguing against."

Serena glared at him. All she really wanted was for Jack to leave. Actually, not entirely true. She wished he'd never been there at all. Because now that he'd been there, in her office, she'd always see him there. Like the ghost of lovers past, he'd haunt her, but she could get beyond that if he would just leave. He wouldn't, though. Not until he was good and ready. She knew that much about him hadn't changed.

Serena also knew exactly what she wanted to say to her brother Bennett, but she couldn't do that until Jack left. And, clearly, the man was going nowhere until he'd told her all about his brilliant *idea*.

"Fine." She hitched one hip higher than the other and tapped the toe of her red heeled sandal against the floor. "Tell me what your *brilliant* idea is."

He held up one finger. "Didn't say brilliant. I said it's a good idea. Plus, it will work for both the Carey Corporation and the Colton Group. It will bring you more donors and more money for the underprivileged kids. That's what it's all about, right?"

She took a deep breath and let it out again. He had a point. "Okay then, tell me."

Jack's mouth curved just a bit and Serena ignored it. Mostly. It wasn't easy because, oh, she had such memories of that luscious mouth of his.

"All right. I'm going to donate stays at Colton Group hotels in a raffle you're going to run."

"What?" She stared at him, waiting for the punch line. "Donating hotel rooms? A raffle? That's the big plan?"

Frowning at her, he said, "Not just hotel rooms. Five-star hotel rooms. I'm donating twelve one-week stays at any of my hotels—here or in Europe— winner's choice, of course. And those weeks are all-inclusive. Meals. Airfare."

Stunned, Serena thought about what he was offering and had to admit that he was right. This kind of prize offering would certainly bring more people out. For the chance to win one of twelve one-week stays at a five-star hotel anywhere in the world, people would be willing to buy a lot of raffle tickets.

After a moment, she asked, "Twelve weeks to one winner, or twelve winners?"

He shrugged. "Up to you, since you're *in charge*. But I would think twelve winners would get the donations rolling in."

She tapped one finger against her bottom lip as her brain began to race with possibilities. Boy, she hated to admit that Jack was right. This was a spectacular prize, and she knew their donors would love it and, more important, *compete* for it. That would result in more money for the foundation and more children would be helped. It was a good idea.

Damn it.

"Agreed. Twelve winners would create more… eagerness." Then she tipped her head to one side and looked up at him. "What do you get out of this, Jack?"

He walked a little closer and Serena deliberately stood her ground. He wasn't that attractive, after all. Okay, yes, he was, but she didn't have to let him know she thought so.

"I've spent the last several years updating our hotels." He looked into her eyes. "The reputation that was fading ten years ago has been fixed. I want to get the word out that a Colton Group hotel is the only one worth staying at." He shrugged. "And I figured this was a damn good place to start."

"You never heard of ad space on TV, radio and online?"

His lips quirked. "What can I say? I like the personal touch. Bottom line is, Bennett wants us to work together to plan it out and set it all up to the best advantage for both of us."

"Work together." Nope, repeating the words didn't help her deal with it.

"Problem?"

"Why would there be a problem?" *So* many problems.

"Excellent." He buttoned his suit jacket and said, "So when do you want to start working on this?"

How about *never*?

"I'll get back to you on that after I talk to Bennett." Stalling wasn't refusing. It was just…putting off the inevitable. Forced to work with the man who had once broken her heart? She wasn't a teenager. She could do that. For the children. But, damn it, Bennett should have talked to her before agreeing to this with Jack.

"Fine. He has my new number. Call me when you're ready to talk." He headed for the door, and when he got there, he paused and looked back at her. "It's good to see you, Serena. I knew it would be."

She didn't answer. Apparently, he didn't require one, because in the next moment he opened the door, walked through it and was gone.

Again.

Two

Walking into Bennett's office, Jack had to silently admit that his meeting with Serena had gone better than he'd thought it would. His old friend was on the phone, so Jack took a moment to look around.

Bennett's office was so different from Serena's it was a wonder they were in the same building. The space was huge, maybe twice the size of Serena's, with a better view and floor-to-ceiling tinted windows making up one wall. The furnishings were sparse but starkly modern, with sharp lines, lots of chrome, glass and leather; it was, Jack thought, completely impersonal. He didn't see one damn thing in the room that reminded him of his friend. What

had probably happened was Bennett hired a decorator who then got it all wrong and he hadn't cared
enough to demand it be changed. That sounded like
Bennett.

"Still alive, I see."

He turned, grinned and watched Bennett hang
up the phone. "A little bruised, but yeah, breathing."

"Was I right?" Bennett leaned back in his desk
chair. "Did she soak you for a table?"

"Yeah, she did. You called that one. Got me for
seventy-five."

Bennett laughed. "That's my sister. Cheer up,
Jack. It's going to a good cause."

"I don't give a damn about the money."

"Times have really changed for you, then," Bennett mused.

Jack dropped into one of the uncomfortable
guest chairs in front of Bennett's desk and looked
at his friend. Bennett was one of the few people
who knew exactly why he'd left the country—and
Serena—seven years before.

Back then, Jack had walked away from Serena
because he'd had no choice. He was in no position
to give her what she wanted. Hell, everything he'd
ever known about marriage had proved it was a
prison until one of the caged fought their way free.
Love hadn't been a part of his lexicon back then
and he wasn't sure it was even now. What was love

but some ephemeral notion that came and went as easily as the breeze off the ocean?

So he'd had to leave. Yeah, he knew he'd hurt her. But if he'd stayed and failed at the future she'd wanted for them, it would have hurt her more. Now he was back because he'd done what he'd needed to do. Proved to himself that he was a better man than his father. Proved that he could save the Colton Group hotel chain in spite of the damage his father had done to it. And maybe, he thought, he was better than the old man at other things, as well. Maybe he could have a relationship without letting it all go to crap.

He hadn't come back *for* Serena. But there was no ignoring her, or avoiding her, come to that. Jack was moving back home for good. And Bennett was his closest friend, so he wouldn't be able to maintain that relationship without seeing Serena. But seven years was a long time and they'd both changed a lot. She'd moved on and he couldn't blame her for it. She was a mother now. Divorced from a dick who hadn't deserved her any more than Jack had.

So even though everything in him had wanted to reach for Serena, he hadn't. He'd lost that right, and judging from the reception she'd given him, he wouldn't be welcome. Although, he mused, he'd expected more ice from her. Had she changed so much that she was able to actually hide her real feelings now? Back in the day, Serena had worn her heart out in the open for everyone to see. Today, he'd had the impression there were millions of thoughts racing through her brain and he wasn't privy to any of them.

But, damn, he couldn't help wanting her. That particular ache had never gone away completely.

So, better that they both get used to being around each other right from the jump.

"Yeah," he said thoughtfully. "Things have changed. Made a ton of changes to the company, got rid of a lot of dead wood at the top, and now the Colton Group is bigger and healthier than ever."

"Your mom still happy with her new husband?" Bennett asked.

"Yeah. John's great for her. Treats her like a queen, and they live in an apartment in Paris that Mom loves. She's happy and settled, so I'm moving back home."

"Good news," Bennett said. He walked across the office to the coffee bar. "Want one?"

"Sure. Black." Jack stood, then walked over to join him. "Serena wasn't exactly thrilled to see me."

Bennett held up one hand. "Nope. I told you seven years ago. No details."

Laughing, Jack took the offered coffee. "Seriously? It's been seven years and you still don't want to know what happened? Still sitting this out?" He took a sip of coffee, then said, "Most brothers are more protective of their sisters."

"Oh, I'm protective," Bennett assured him, but shook his head at the same time. "But I learned my lesson with Amanda ten years ago. Got involved then and only made things worse. So when you and Serena broke up, I stepped back."

Jack nodded. "Whatever the reason, I appreciate it."

"Oh, hell, I didn't do it for you." Laughing, Bennett said, "I did it for my own sake. The mess with Amanda and Henry Porter might have turned out differently if I hadn't gotten involved. But just so you know, that doesn't mean I won't do it again if I have to."

Jack studied his friend for a long minute before he simply said, "Understood."

Hell, he'd known that coming home again wouldn't be easy, but seeing Serena again, feeling the ice of her, hadn't been pretty, though he'd known she wouldn't exactly greet him with open arms. Still, she hadn't thrown anything at him, so maybe he should consider that a win.

"Working with her won't be a problem?"

Jack looked at him and lied. "No. Not at all." Then, in a sudden change of subject, he added, "While I'm here. What do you think about working up a package between my hotel and your restaurant?"

Confusion shone in Bennett's eyes. "You mean besides the prizes you're offering at the benefit?"

"Yeah." Actually, Jack had been doing a lot of thinking about these things. "This is separate from the gala."

Bennett frowned, but motioned with one hand for Jack to go on.

With Serena pushed to the back of his mind, where, he told himself, she should stay, Jack said, "The Colton Dana Point hotel is going to have a big reopen by the end of the month. I've been renovating—"

"Yeah, I've seen the construction crews on my drive to work."

He laughed. "Yeah, well, they're nearly done. Just putting some finishing touches on and the decorators are wrapping things up on the penthouse level this week." Jack took a sip of coffee and wandered to the windows overlooking the greenbelt. It was a nice enough view, but too many office buildings for his tastes. That was why he'd moved his headquarters to Newport Beach, where he could watch the ocean from his office.

When he'd lived in Europe, he'd always managed to get a view of the Atlantic, but the Pacific was home. And looking at it reminded him of how far he'd come and, now that he was home again, how much more he still had to accomplish. Jack had vowed to take the family company to the top of the food chain and he wouldn't stop until he had. He'd watched his father nearly destroy the very thing that he and his mother had depended on. Jack would never again trust his mother's well-being or his own to anyone but himself.

The idea he wanted to run past Bennett wasn't designed to be a game changer at all, but Jack figured it was a good way to reintroduce the Colton hotels to Orange County. Turning to face Bennett, he said, "I'm thinking that we offer our guests coupons for dinner at your restaurant and having you offer coupons for my hotel. Gain both of us some business."

Bennett leaned against the coffee bar and thought about it. Hell, Jack could practically see the wheels turning in the man's head. "You know the Carey restaurant is a five-star operation."

"So's my hotel. What's your point?"

Bennett snorted. "Are you talking a permanent sort of arrangement?"

"Not thinking that far down the road, actually," Jack said. "I see this as a trial period for now. I'm thinking we can offer a one-night stay at our hotel and a dinner for two at your restaurant. Hell, your restaurant's in Laguna, just a short drive from my hotel, so it would work out well for both of us. And maybe we'll both get guests we might not have otherwise."

"It's an intriguing idea," Bennett mused. "Why don't we talk about it over lunch?"

"At your restaurant?"

"You know a better one?"

"Well," Jack said, "I have been gone for seven years. Maybe there is a better one now."

Bennett grinned. "There isn't."

"Just what I wanted to hear."

"One thing we don't talk about," Bennett said as he set his coffee cup aside. "Serena."

Hell, Jack didn't even want to think about Serena at the moment, so that stipulation worked for him. Besides, what was between him and Serena should *stay* between him and Serena.

"Agreed," he said tightly.

"What is this? Reunion Romance Spring?" Amanda Carey's voice hitched higher and Serena shushed her sister.

She glanced around the Carey Center Pavilion, then back to Amanda. "Can you keep your voice down?" It probably wouldn't help, since the acoustics in the pavilion were every bit as exceptional as those in the concert hall itself.

While the Carey Concert Hall was the star of the Carey Center, the pavilion was rented out for wedding receptions, family gatherings and, in this case, the annual gala. The room itself was cavernous, with some of the same decorative points used in the concert hall. Lots of glass and gold and chrome, with a gleaming polished oak floor and overhead chandeliers that made that floor sparkle like a jewel. The walls were mostly floor-to-ceiling windows, which afforded views of the gardens that surrounded the building. And now, in the heart of spring, the trees were in full bloom and the roses were just coming into their own.

The night of the gala, those accordion-style windows would be opened to the night air, allowing the scents of the garden to swamp the pavilion, adding another layer of romance to the night. For the gala itself, part of the room would be used for dancing, while high-top tables dotted the rest of the space. There would be chairs scattered throughout for people to rest when they needed to, but usually, people wandered, visited and danced the night away.

Today, she'd come here with Amanda to lay it all out in her mind, along with the changes she'd put into place. Of course, the flowers, the catering stations and the tables and chairs weren't there, but in her mind's eye, Serena could see it all as it would be.

Of course, the gala plans weren't uppermost in her mind at the moment. "This is not a romantic reunion, and for heaven's sake, keep it down."

"Lower my voice?" Amanda said, laughing. "Sure. My reaction is what's weird here." Shaking her head, Amanda walked to the closest accordion window group and opened it to let an ocean breeze slide inside. "Suddenly I'm wishing we could have a glass of wine in the middle of a workday."

"Probably better this way," Serena said. "After talking to Jack, I'd need a bottle or two, and that would solve nothing."

"Fine. No wine." Amanda stepped outside and lifted her face to the sun. "If it's not a big romantic reunion—and let me tell you, they're very nice—"

Serena rolled her eyes. Ever since Amanda and her Henry had reconnected, and now become engaged, she never missed the chance to tell her sister all about how happy she was. Not that Serena begrudged her or anything, but this wasn't about Amanda.

"So, tell me why he's here."

"How do I know?" Serena gave up even the pretense of normal.

Serena followed her sister outside and crossed her arms over her middle as if giving herself a comforting hug. Naturally, it didn't help. Ordinarily, she loved the gardens at the center. Serena couldn't keep a plant alive, so being there with the scents and colors was sort of soothing, and definitely calming on a typical crazy Carey family day. But today she wasn't feeling it.

Her stomach felt as jumpy as the jittery beat of her heart. Sighing, she said, "Amanda, it was so weird to just look up and see Jack standing there in my doorway. And worse? He says he's moving back to California permanently."

"Yes, but what I want to know is, how's he look?"

Serena's eyebrows lifted. "Really? That's what you want to know? What he looks like?"

"Shoot me," her sister quipped. "I'm shallow that way."

Serena huffed out an exasperated breath. "How do you think?"

Amanda sighed. "Probably great."

"Bingo." Somehow, he'd managed to get even more handsome over the last seven years. Back when she loved him, Serena had thought he was the most gorgeous man she'd ever seen. A sardonic smile, a flash in his beautiful eyes and just a hint of recklessness that drew her in even when it shouldn't have. Today, she'd seen all that and more in him.

That fact was extremely annoying.

"Too bad he didn't develop a limp or something," Amanda mused.

Serena smiled. It was nice to know her sister and she were on the same page here. "Just what I thought. But, sadly, he didn't. Now he's back and says he's only going to Europe on business trips now."

"Okay…" Amanda sat on one of the decorative iron benches scattered throughout the gardens. Draping one arm along the back, she looked up at her sister. "But just because he's moving back here doesn't mean you have to be around him."

Serena dropped down beside her. "He's one of Bennett's best friends."

"True."

"And he bought a table at the gala."

"Okay, well, that makes a statement. He spent fifty thousand just to see you."

"Not just to see me," Serena corrected. "And it was seventy-five, actually. I charged him extra. I shouldn't have, but—"

"Are you kidding?" Amanda gave a delighted laugh. "You should have charged him even more."

"Thanks." Good to have family on your side when you needed them, Serena thought. But it still didn't solve her problem. "He's going to be there. At the gala. In my life. Driving me crazy."

"You're not still in love with him, are you?"

"Of course not," she assured Amanda. "That would make me a complete fool. He walked out on me the minute I told him I loved him." And she hadn't said a word. Hadn't fought back or forced him to tell her why he was leaving. She'd simply stood there and taken it. Well, she wasn't that quiet, timid woman anymore. "I got over him. Married Robert. Had Alli. I totally moved on, so why on earth would I still care about Jack?"

"You shouldn't."

"Exactly." She nodded to herself and stiffened her spine. She was long since over the man she'd once loved so desperately. Even remembering her feelings at the time now embarrassed her. She'd been so sure the night she told him that she loved him. So positive that he would say those words back to her. That they would plan a future together.

And then none of it had happened.

She'd watched his eyes and seen the distance that had sprung up in those dark blue depths almost instantly. Serena had known that this wasn't going to be the fairy-tale ending she wanted so badly. He'd kissed her, told her he couldn't be what she wanted and left so quickly it was a wonder he hadn't left a Jack-sized hole in her front door. And she'd been so damn shattered by that action she'd married the first jerk who'd come along. Robert O'Dare had been a terrible husband, but at least with him, she'd finally discovered her spine. She had Jack to thank for that, as well.

And until today, she hadn't seen him again. She didn't want to remember the rush of heat that had swamped her or the quick jump of her heartbeat when he walked into her office so unexpectedly. Except for the occasional guest spot in her dreams, Jack had been invisible for seven years. She'd been married—granted, to a man who had made her life a misery—and she had a child. Alli was the light of her life. Basically, in the last seven years, Serena had watched her life crash and burn. Then she'd rebuilt it from the ashes, and now she was finally on a path that was one she'd forged herself.

She didn't need or want Jack Colton to push himself back into her life and throw everything off balance again.

"So you didn't get excited when you saw him?"

"No." *Yes*.

"Uh-huh." Amanda studied her manicure for a second or two. "I don't believe that for a second."

"Well, you could pretend and help *me* pretend."

"What's the point of that?" Amanda shook her head, gave Serena a one-armed hug and sat back to look at her again. "We both know that Jack Colton is your kryptonite. So it's better if you just admit it going in and then promise yourself that you're going to ignore it."

"Doesn't sound better to me," Serena admitted. "How can it be good to say yes, he still does it for me, but I'm not going to do anything about it?"

"Because then it's just your willpower against the sexual pull."

"Uh-huh." Serena stared her sister down. "Right. So I should ignore that pull as well as you did with Henry?"

Frowning, Amanda muttered, "That's different."

"Sure it is."

Just last month, Henry Porter, Amanda's long-lost love, had appeared again after being gone for ten years. And like metal filings to a magnet, the two of them were drawn together, in spite of their shared past, and now they were engaged.

Serena was happy for her sister, but Amanda was right, too. Their situations couldn't be more different. Fighting a sexual pull was going to be a full-time job, since she and Jack would be seeing a lot of each other, and she had no doubt it would be the most difficult one she'd ever done. But she couldn't fail. Couldn't risk letting her life be destroyed again. Especially by a gorgeous man who knew how to push all her buttons.

"Okay, fine. The situation is different. But," Amanda added, "sounds like Jack's here to stay, so you're going to have to find a way to deal with him."

"Do I?" Serena pushed off the bench, took a few steps, then whirled around again. "Just because he's back in the States doesn't mean we have to see each other." Thinking about that, she mused aloud, "Although he is friends with Bennett, but then, how much time does Bennett spend with his friends? He's more obsessed with the business than Dad is."

"Speaking of Dad," Amanda interrupted, "not that I'm finished talking about this, but Mom stopped in to see me this morning after she left you."

Serena sighed. "I'm sorry about sending her off to you. But, really, I'd had enough *help*."

"No problem, really. Well," she hedged, "not much of one. But the thing is, Mom says that Dad backed out of their trip to San Francisco."

Rolling her eyes in exasperation, Serena said, "Mom didn't take that well, I'm guessing."

"You could say that," Amanda told her. "Mom says she's going on the trip alone and staying at a different hotel than their usual so that if Dad does decide to follow her, he won't be able to find her."

"This is starting to feel like a soap opera."

"Starting to?" Amanda pushed her hair back when the breeze blew it across her eyes. "If Dad doesn't keep his promise to retire soon, I don't know what's going to happen."

"Great. This is just great."

"Honestly," Amanda said, "I shouldn't be happy about that, but I sort of am. At least it means three days of peace."

"Does it? All it really means is that Dad will be bugging us, not Mom."

"Good point." Amanda nodded and sighed. "Okay, back to Jack."

"No." Serena shook her head, set her hands at her hips and took a deep breath. "I'm done with Jack. What we had ended seven years ago. Nothing can change that." She lifted her chin, squared her shoulders and said, "I've got my job, my house, and most especially, I've got Alli. I'm fine. I like my life just as it is, and I don't need Jack in it."

"Right. So you're just going to be supermom and never be with another man?"

"How's my track record with men?" Serena asked, not needing an answer. "Jack left me. Robert married me to use me. Does it sound like I should be out choosing *another* man? No," she answered before Amanda could. "That way lies madness. Besides, I like standing on my own. I'm a mom. I make the decisions for Alli and I don't have any interest in letting a man in on that."

"Right." Amanda stood up, dropped her hands on her sister's shoulders and stared into her eyes. "Okay, sweetie, here's the thing. You need more than Alli and your job. You always have. You're the one who always dreamed of being a wife and a mom."

"I know, but things change." It was true. She'd never wanted the competitive world of the Careys. Yet here she was now, taking her place in the family business. And, damn it, she was good at the job, too. She was finding her niche. So if that much had changed, what else was possible? Maybe one day, she'd be the CEO of the Carey Corporation. She could unseat Bennett and wouldn't that be fun?

Even as she considered the possibilities, Serena dismissed them. "No," she said, with a firm shake of her head. Maybe she wasn't totally in love with the corporate life, but... "I always wanted family,

I give you that. But I realized something a couple of months ago."

Amanda sighed and smiled. "Okay, let's hear the epiphany that's going to keep you a vestal virgin."

Serena laughed. "The virgin ship sailed a long time ago. All I've really discovered is I don't need another man in my life, because I've already got family."

"Sweetie…"

"No, hear me out." Serena looked around the garden, noticing two of the gardening crew working in the distance. The glass on the concert hall gleamed in the sun, a soft breeze carried the scent of the ocean, and here she stood in the middle of it all with her sister. Things could be worse. "Working at the company, I have time with my sister, my brothers—when Justin bothers to show up—and my parents, as irritating as that can be sometimes."

"It's not the same thing as having your own family," Amanda said softly. "I was busy burying myself in the family business, too, remember? Then Henry came back into my life and I realized what was missing."

She gave her a smile. Amanda just didn't understand that for Serena that longing was over. She'd wanted it, briefly had it, then lost it all. Now there was more than just her heart to worry about, and she wouldn't risk Alli caring for a man in their lives only to lose him and have her heart broken, too.

"I'm glad you and Henry are together again and that you're engaged and all set up for a happily-ever-after," Serena said, meaning every word. "But it's not for me." Amanda opened her mouth to speak, but Serena cut her off. "Don't look so stricken. I'm fine. I'm actually happy. For the first time in my life, I'm making my own happiness. I'm finding out that I'm good at my job, I have my family, and most important, I have Alli."

Her daughter was the one good thing that had come from her short-lived and unlamented marriage. Her ex had turned out to be a horrible human who'd only married her to worm his way into the Carey family's wealth. He'd cheated on her almost from the first, though she'd been the clueless wife. So wrapped up in her own vision of what she and Robert were, she missed all the signs that were, in retrospect, so obvious.

And by the time she'd discovered the truth about Robert, Serena was pregnant. With Bennett's help, she divorced him, got Robert to sign a document relinquishing all rights to their child and began the task of building a life for her and her daughter.

Now life was nearly perfect and would only get better as she got stronger. Why would she want to risk it all on the chance of maybe, at some point, possibly being in love?

Nope.

"So what you're saying is, you're just going to devote yourself to work and your daughter?"

"Is that so bad?"

"No, but it's what you used to complain about. How Dad and Bennett and *I* were too focused on work."

"Yes, but—"

"And counting on Alli to make you happy outside of work puts a lot of pressure on her, doesn't it?"

"Of course it would, but I'm not doing that." Was she?

"Not yet," Amanda said. "But eventually, if you don't have another outlet besides work, you will."

Frowning, Serena stared off into the distance, letting her sister's warning slide through her mind. Maybe that could happen. But it wouldn't. Not to her. "You're grasping."

"No, I'm not, but maybe you should."

Shaking her head, she asked, "What are you talking about now?"

"I'm talking about you doing a little *grasping* once in a while. Jack showing up is handy, but if you don't want to restart things there—"

"And I don't."

"Fine. All I'm saying is find a guy. Date. Have a complete life."

That was annoying. "For starters, I already have

a complete life, and since when are you a big believer in having a man means completion?"

"I'm not. I'm saying it's what *you* have always thought."

"And that's what led me to Robert, and now I'm over it." She started back inside the pavilion. "Can we move on?"

"Can you? Good question," Amanda mused.

It was, wasn't it?

Three

"I can't believe you're doing this."

Bennett Carey looked up from the paperwork strewn across his desk. "I don't see why not. It's an excellent addition to the gala, and if the Carey Corporation owned spectacular hotels, I'd offer them up, too." He sat back in his chair, steepled his fingers in front of him and tipped his head to one side to study her. "The idea's a good one and you know it. Jack gets some great publicity for the new hotels and we get the added bonus of extra donations to the fundraiser. Work with Jack to set it all up in time."

Serena just stared at him. Oh, she would work with Jack…because clearly she had to. And like she'd told Amanda, she was completely over him. But that didn't mean she wasn't going to confront Bennett about setting her up without even *warning* her what he was going to do.

Bennett bent his head and went back to work as if she'd already hurried from the room to carry out his orders. "Work with Jack."

"Yes."

"And you didn't think you should talk to me about this?"

"Seriously?" He dropped his pen to the desktop and looked up at her again, impatience clear on his features. "It was seven years ago, Serena. You've been married and divorced. You have a daughter. Are you actually trying to tell me you're not over Jack Colton yet?"

"I didn't say that," she argued. "Look at you. You're still furious with Henry Porter and it's been ten years, not to mention he's now engaged to Amanda."

He scowled at her.

"And of course I'm over him. I just don't want to work with him."

"Get over that, too," he advised.

"I'm touched, Bennett, by the brotherly concern."

He dropped his pen, sat back in his chair and stared up at her. "Oh, I'm concerned—that you're acting as if you can't handle your job when it comes with a little conflict."

"Ha!" Her laugh was short and sharp. *This* was what she was fighting against. The you-can't-do-it thing from her own brother, for heaven's sake. Partly her own fault since she'd spent so many years avoiding the very business she was now devoting herself to. But times changed. *She* had changed and she would make them all see it, sooner or later. "I can't handle my job? Since when? You haven't had any complaints about the work I'm doing, have you?"

He stared at her. "No. Of course not."

Nodding, she took a step closer to his desk. "That's right, you haven't, and yet the first thing you say is that I can't handle my job when it comes with a little conflict. Well, in case you haven't noticed, the Carey family is filled with conflict and I do just fine, thanks."

"I didn't say you couldn't handle it," he said slowly. "I said you were *acting* as if you couldn't handle it. Big difference."

Maybe he had a point.

"Fine. My point is, I simply don't think it's necessary to import conflict."

Bennett grinned. "Good one. Look, Jack's a good guy. You guys had issues. Fine. It's done. This is a good idea for both of our companies. Make it happen, Serena. After all, you don't want Jack to think you can't handle being around him, right?"

She hadn't considered that and scowled at her brother. "Low blow, but I get your meaning. Fine.

I'll handle it. But if anything like this comes up again…"

"A warning. Agreed."

"That's all I want." Well, not *all*. But close enough for now.

That evening, Serena picked Alli up from the company day care and took her to the Summer Sensation auditions at the Carey Center. Every year, the Carey Center held a series of summer concerts that was very popular. But this year, they were adding a new element. They were holding auditions for a contest called Summer Stars. And every act that auditioned would be recorded and added to the Carey Center website, where the public could vote for their favorites. At the end of the contest, the winner would be awarded a chance to shine for one night during the Summer Sensation concert series.

The response from the public had been overwhelming and now they were holding open auditions every night at the center. Like a television reality show, there were some people who had no business being on a stage, and a few others who were born to be stars. Even Serena had gotten caught up in the magic and the dreams and went to the auditions most nights.

Sitting in the Carey Center with her family, watching people chase their dreams, was…wonderful. She admired them all. Even those with no talent, only the ambition to be rich and famous. Because every one of them had put it all on the line to try for what they wanted.

"Can I sing, too, Mommy?"

She looked down at her daughter and smiled into those big blue eyes. Amazing that just being with her little girl could make the worst day better. "Sure, sweetie. We'll sing in the car all the way home, okay?"

Alli clutched her doll a little tighter and did a sort of hopping step beside Serena as they made their way down the center aisle to where her family was sitting. The sound of those joyful little steps was almost lost in the cavernous glory of the Carey Center.

This building was designed to celebrate the arts and no one did it better.

There were three levels of seating, fronted by glass railings that rippled like waves on the ocean. Those rails were wrapped around an oak stage where the honey-colored wood was polished to a gleam that rivaled a mirror. The stage was seventy feet wide and fifty deep, perfect for a complete orchestra, a huge choir or an intricate ballet.

Every red velvet seat in the house had a wonderful view of the performance, and the ceiling was studded with crystals that looked, with the reflected lighting, like stars on a black sky.

The hall itself sat two thousand, not counting

the five private boxes and other VIP seating. Back-stage, there were several dressing rooms and a lux-uriously appointed performers' lounge, where the stars of the evening could relax before and after the show with their friends and families.

The lobby of the center was elegant, with miles of Spanish tiles and acres of glass and chrome. There was a café for refreshments, a gift shop and a first-aid station, just in case.

For now, though, the center was mostly empty but for the front row, where audition contestants for the night and their friends nervously awaited their turn in the spotlight.

Halfway up the main aisle, Candace Carey waited, beaming a smile at her only grandchild.

"Nana!" Alli shouted in excitement, broke away from Serena and ran the rest of the distance to throw herself at her grandmother.

"Hi, peanut," Candace said, bending down to scoop the little girl up into her arms. Looking over Alli's head, she said, "Serena, it's so good to see you here. We have a couple of exciting performers tonight and I can't wait to hear your opinion."

"Sure, Mom." While Alli and Candace began their mutual-admiration meeting, Serena took a seat behind Amanda, leaned forward and whis-pered, "Sorry?"

Amanda turned around to face her, glanced at their mother, who was spinning in circles with

Alli, and then grinned at Serena. "No reason to be sorry," she said in a hurried whisper. "I actually handed off the auditions to Mom."

"You're kidding!" Okay, she hadn't expected that.

"Oh, no." Amanda shook her head. "I've got so much to do arranging the performances for Summer Sensation—and another one of our regulars is making noises about better compensation—"

"They want more money?" That surprised Serena. Performers at the Carey Center were some of the best paid in the country.

"Oh, no, they want a specific *meal* and snacks set out in the performers' lounge—snacks before the performance and a hot meal after. And not just any dinner, either. They want it catered by the Carey restaurant."

"Wow. Picky. Though," Serena noted with a shrug, "they have good taste. Our restaurant is wonderful."

"True, but I've never had to negotiate steaks in a contract." She sighed a little and continued, "And besides all of that, I've got a brand-new fiancé I'd like to spend some time with." She paused and took a breath. "Anyway, Mom had a couple of good ideas for the Summer Stars competition, and she's looking for something to do because Dad's driving her nuts, so I handed it off to her."

"And she's good with that?"

"Are you kidding? She's thrilled." Amanda

glanced at their mom. "She's already working with the web designer to get the audition tapes online. Tomorrow she's meeting with the tabulation experts about setting up the voting. Honestly, Serena, Mom's doing a great job."

Serena wasn't even sure why she was surprised. Candace Carey had raised four kids and helped her husband build the center into what it was today. Just because the woman *wanted* to retire and go on adventures with her husband didn't mean she was incapable of doing the work. "Okay then, I feel no guilt for tossing her at you."

"None at all. I only came tonight to be with her on her first night heading the auditions. But it's not like she needs me."

As if to prove it, Candace held on to Alli and walked down toward the stage. She spoke to the pianist and the cameramen and then headed back up the aisle, with Alli skipping beside her. "Okay, girls, we're ready for our first competitor tonight." She checked her tablet and said, "Jacob Foley, a guitarist, and his sister Sheila, singing."

Amanda winced and Serena couldn't blame her. They'd both sat through several family acts that had been... *Disappointing* was a good word.

"Oh, don't look so appalled," Candace said, a laugh in her voice. "Earlier, I heard them rehearsing backstage, and they were wonderful."

Serena called Alli to her, because if the auditions

were truly awful, she'd just take her daughter and go home. Dragging her little girl up onto her lap, Serena whispered, "Shh, let's listen to the music."

"Singing?" Alli clapped her hands.

"We hope so, sweetie," Amanda whispered from in front of her.

"Hush now." Candace fixed her daughters with a stern stare, then winked at her granddaughter before turning her attention to the stage.

The lighting manager focused a soft pale blue spotlight on the center of the stage. A man, about thirty, holding a guitar and a younger woman carrying a violin stepped into that light and without pausing a moment began to play. It sounded Celtic to Serena and automatically her toe began to tap to the quick, lively music. Alli clapped along, and when the fiddle player lowered her violin and added her voice to the song, it was magic. Serena was completely caught up in the moment, and one look at her mother told her she wasn't the only one.

The music came to an abrupt—almost startling— end and Serena wasn't alone in applauding.

"They were amazing," Amanda said, as they watched the Foley family rush the stage to congratulate the two performers.

"Just wonderful!" Candace gave a happy sigh and laid one hand against her chest for dramatic effect. "Oh, I can't wait to see that performance up on the website. I'm sure they'll get hundreds of votes."

"Mom, I'm so impressed with you—talking websites!"

"Thanks!" Candace grinned. "You know, it's not as confusing as I thought it would be. After all, I don't have to design them. I just have to tell those who do what I want."

"That's great, Mom, seriously."

Candace shot a sardonic look at Amanda. "Yes, I'm sure you're happy, dear. Mom's out of your hair and actually doing well."

Amanda winced. "Out of my hair is a little strong."

"But accurate?"

"Mom…" Serena felt obliged to defend her sister.

Candace laughed and waved one hand. "Oh, relax, both of you. I know when I'm bugging my kids. But it was worth it, because I'm having fun with my new job."

"I'm glad," Amanda said. "And you really are helping me out, Mom. Between the Summer Sensation and planning the wedding, I've hardly got time to see Henry."

On the stage, people were moving things into place, getting ready for the next performance.

"Can't have that, can we?" Candace turned her gaze on Serena. "And what about you, honey? I hear Jack Colton is back."

"Really, Mom?" Serena rolled her eyes. "You, too?"

"Nana, too, what?" Alli asked.

"Me, too, a little nosy, sweet girl," Candace said and tapped the little girl's nose. Lifting her gaze to Serena, she said, "Well, Serena?"

"Well what?" A little exasperated, she countered, "He came in to see Bennett and he had an idea for the gala, so he stopped by my office to see me about it and that's the end of it."

At the front of the hall, the Foleys were still accepting congratulations for their performance and handing over their contact information to the web designer.

"Shouldn't you go and check on the next act to audition?"

"There's time," Candace said with a wink for Amanda. "So are you going to see him again?"

"About the gala? You bet. For anything else, not a chance," Serena assured her. Dipping her head, Serena kissed Alli's cheek. "What about it, sweet girl? Want to stop on the way home and get some ice cream?"

"Yay!" Alli jumped up and raced into the center aisle, where she hopped up and down on tiny pink tennies.

"You guys have fun," Serena said, more than happy to escape any more conversations about Jack. "We're going home."

"Then it seems I'm just in time to walk you to your car."

Serena's heart actually *sank*. Funny, she'd never really understood that expression until that very moment. So slowly it was almost as if she weren't moving at all, Serena turned to face Jack Colton standing beside her brother Bennett.

"This place is even more amazing than I remembered," Jack said, glancing around the concert hall before looking at Serena.

"Well, thank you." Candace spoke up to fill the sudden silence. "It's nice to see you again, Jack. Are you and Bennett here to watch the auditions with me?"

"I am," Bennett said, dropping into the closest seat. "I want to make sure you're not feeling overwhelmed by the job Amanda handed off." He frowned at his sister and she stuck her tongue out at him.

"I'm not overwhelmed. I'm just fine."

"Good, good," Bennett said, pulling his phone out of his pocket and turning it on. "Jack's not here to watch the auditions. He just stopped in to—" He cut off, turned to look at his friend and said, "Why did you stop by?"

"Seemed like a good idea at the time." His eyes were fixed on Serena and she felt the power of that stare right down to her bones. "Haven't seen this place in years, so when you were coming, thought I'd go with you."

"There you have it," Bennett said and settled into checking his email.

He just dropped by? Serena wasn't buying that for a second. But he couldn't have known she'd be there. So what was he up to? And, more important, why did she care?

"Okay, well, Alli and I are heading out," she announced. "You guys enjoy the auditions." She picked up her purse, her sweater and then took Alli's hand as she stepped into the aisle.

"Oh, I'll walk with you," Jack said, and she didn't even stop.

"Thanks, but not necessary."

"What's your name?" Alli asked, looking around her mother to the man walking beside her.

He smiled down at her. "My name's Jack, pretty girl. And you're Alli, aren't you?"

Her eyes went wide. "You know me?"

"I sure do," he said, then smiled at her mother. "Your mommy and I have been *friends* for a long time."

"I like friends," Alli mused with what Serena thought was almost a flirtatious smile. Honestly, Jack appealed to women of all ages. In reaction, Serena quickened her steps up the aisle, hoping that Jack would take a hint and just leave them alone. Of course, he didn't.

"We can be friends, too," Jack said, and he was rewarded with a grin.

"Well, that's very nice," Serena said briskly, "but you really don't have to walk us to my car, Jack. Alli and I are fine, aren't we, sweetie?"

"We're getting ice cream!"

Serena sighed.

"I like ice cream," Jack said.

"You want some with us?" Alli asked.

"I'd love some, if it's all right with your mom."

"'Cause we're friends."

"And friends have ice cream," Serena muttered, knowing when she was beaten. She looked down at her daughter's smiling face and knew there was no way to refuse. For whatever reason, Alli had decided that Jack was going to be her buddy. "Okay, let's go."

Jack smiled. Alli celebrated with a quick dance and Serena wondered how she'd lost control of the situation.

Jack hadn't really expected to spend time with Serena and her daughter. But he wasn't complaining.

The nostalgic ice-cream shop boasted small round tables, tiny uncomfortable chairs and a black-and-white-checked floor. The servers were impossibly cheery, but the ice cream was delicious. The company even more so.

"You two must come here a lot," he said. "The girl behind the counter knew Alli's favorite."

"It's only a few blocks from our condo, so yes," Serena said. "We are here a lot."

"It's good!" Alli said firmly as she took another lick at her cone.

Jack smiled at the little girl, then studied Serena over his chocolate-chip cone and took his time with both. Her honey-colored hair was just shoulder length and her blue eyes were as deep as he remembered. She wore a long-sleeved dark scarlet dress with a tight skirt and some red high heels, and every time her tongue stroked her ice cream, he felt that action pounding in his bloodstream.

He hadn't come back to the States *for* her, but he had to admit to himself just how good it was to see her again. Hell, a part of him had thought that seeing her again would be no big deal. That seven years was long enough to cool any feelings he'd once had for her. He'd thought only to come back home. To be a part of things again.

Now that he'd seen Serena, though, talked to her, he could silently admit that there was still... heat. And want.

Just to watch her eyes flash when she was annoyed. To see that soft smile curve her mouth— even when the smile was directed at her daughter, not him. Hell, the woman could still intrigue him with a glance and he hadn't expected that at all. Nor did he know what the hell to do with it. Once upon a time, all Serena had wanted was to fall in love, have a family and be happy.

And she'd wanted all of that with him.

Seven years ago, all of her dreams had sounded like a life sentence to Jack. And when she'd turned those big blue eyes on him and told him she loved him… Hell, he couldn't leave town fast enough. He wasn't proud of it, but it was something he'd had to do. Not just for his own sake, either, though that was clearly how it had looked to Serena and everybody else. But for her sake, too. He would have made a miserable husband and he had no interest in being a father. So what she'd wanted wasn't in the cards for the two of them, and it was better that he leave quickly so she didn't waste time spinning fantasies about the two of them.

Maybe he hadn't handled it the right way, but he knew that he'd done the right thing. For both of them. He'd saved his family's company and his mom and Serena. And now Serena had somehow become…*more* than she had been back in the day.

Young Serena had been all dreams and plans, but this Serena had been tested. That had given her a kind of strength her younger self hadn't had. Her eyes were still beautiful, but now he read shadows of pain there. She was a mother, and every time she looked at her child, Jack saw her soften, and he knew that whatever else had happened in the last seven years, that little girl was her mother's heart.

"And then," Alli said, kicking her tennies against the rungs of the chair, "I cried 'cause my magic shoe got dirty, but Miss Ellen cleaned it."

"Magic shoe?" Jack asked, realizing he'd missed most of what had apparently been a very long story.

Nodding, she licked at her ice cream. "Mommy says magic shoes make you happy."

"Ah." He looked at Serena and his eyebrows lifted. "Magic?"

"Gray suede boots are my magic shoes." Primly, she licked at her chocolate-chip cone again and he wondered if she knew what she was doing to him.

He shifted in his seat to ease his discomfort, then concentrated on the back-and-forth between Serena and her daughter. He'd never spent much time around kids, but this one was full of charm.

"Erin's mommy is so happy she made cookies and brought them in today to school."

"Very nutritious day," Serena said wryly. "Cookies *and* ice cream."

"Yes, and maybe more tomorrow. Erin says she's getting a new daddy and her mommy sings at home all the time. And she makes lots of cookies and other good stuff."

"Does she want a new daddy?" Jack asked.

"Oh, yes. Her other one went away like my daddy did, but Mommy says it's okay because we're perfect just us two, but I think I might like a daddy like Erin's getting."

Serena shot Jack a quick look, as if expecting to see pity in his eyes. He didn't give her that, though. Instead, he stared into her eyes and let her see the heat boiling inside him. In response, a flash of that same heat lit up her blue eyes, momentarily. For that one split second, their gazes locked and a soul-searing warmth he hadn't thought to feel again spilled through Jack. When she licked her ice cream again, he damn near groaned.

Then she looked away and focused on her daughter when Alli asked, "When do I get a new daddy?"

"Well, I don't know, baby," Serena said and completely avoided looking at Jack now. And he knew that she was wishing he were anywhere but there at that moment.

Jack, though, was enjoying himself.

"Erin's new daddy made her a castle in their backyard." Alli shot a sly look at Jack. "Can you make a castle?"

Suddenly, he felt as though his measure was being taken by a three-year-old. And, worse, he didn't think he was coming off real well. "I don't know," he admitted. "I've never tried."

"I bet you could," Alli mused.

"We don't have a backyard," her mother reminded her.

Alli sighed and looked at Jack. "We have a roof."

Serena choked out a laugh. "You little traitor. You love the roof garden!"

Sadly, the little girl shook her head. "Doesn't have a castle."

Jack chuckled. "Boy, she's good."

"You have no idea," Serena said, and the dazzle they'd shared a moment ago slipped into a companionable smile from her as if they were sharing a secret. Damned if he didn't enjoy that smile almost as much as the heat. A moment later, though, she must have realized what she was doing, because she allowed the smile to slide from her face. "Now that you're back, where are you staying?" she asked abruptly.

He glanced at her. "At the house."

"Really? You didn't sell it when you left the country?" She stopped, then nodded. "Never mind. I do remember you left in a hurry."

He inclined his head. "Nice hit."

"Thank you."

"But you're right. I guess I did." He took a bite of his strawberry ice cream. "No. I didn't sell the place. Guess I always figured to come back at some point."

Besides, the Colton family home sat on a cliffside in Laguna and had been there for nearly a hundred years. Jack's great-grandfather had built the original house because his wife had always wanted to live where she could watch the sea from her bedroom. Of course, that house had grown and expanded, stretching out across a huge plot of land, and it was more or less a landmark.

The beach community had grown up around the house, though the Colton place maintained a lot of land and a private beach. The house had been up-dated across the years and remodeled whenever the mood struck, but its cedar planking and miles of glass were as much a tradition in the Colton fam-ily as the Carey Center was to the Careys.

"You should come by sometime. See what's changed."

She laughed a little. "Sure. I'll do that."

"We don't have to be enemies, Serena," he said.

"'Cause we're friends," Alli shouted.

"Exactly," Jack said, smiling at the girl.

Serena sighed and shook her head. "Stop charm-ing her."

"Am I?" he asked.

"Do *you* have a backyard?" Alli wondered.

"Alli!" Serena faced her daughter and said, "Jack is not going to build you a castle at his house."

"But he could if he wanted…"

He had to admire the little girl's never-give-up attitude.

Still, Serena changed the subject quickly. "Did it feel strange to be back? Here, I mean. In Cali-fornia. And the family house."

"Not completely." He studied her. "Being back at the house feels right, but I'll admit I didn't know how facing you was going to go."

Her lips curved and he couldn't tear his gaze from her. "I worried you?"

"Not worry," he said. "Let's say…concerned."

She looked pleased at that admission. "Isn't that a nice thing to say."

"What, Mommy? Is Jack nice?"

"He's being very nice at the moment."

"Because we're friends."

"That's right, baby," Serena said and reached over to swipe orange sherbet off the girl's chin.

As the outsider, Jack watched mother and daughter and felt just the tiniest twinge of…something. He wasn't sure he wanted to identify the feeling, so he let it go and concentrated instead on controlling his purely physical responses to Serena.

"I like Jack," Alli said, capturing his attention.

"Well, thank you," he said, grinning at the tiny heartbreaker. "I like you, too."

"That's great. We're all friends." Serena sighed. "Okay, baby girl, now that we've had ice cream, I think it's time we head home."

Alli tipped her head to one side. "Can Jack come?"

Oh, maybe he should build the girl a castle. She was working on her mother for him and no one could have done it better. He looked at Alli and grinned. A moment later, he looked at her mother. "We do have a lot to do about the promotion at the gala," he suggested.

"But not tonight," Serena countered. "And not at my home."

Couldn't blame her for that, but the twinge of

disappointment that pinged inside him was hard to ignore. But, hell, there was always… "Tomorrow?"

At the irritation that bloomed on her features, he only said, "Look, we may not want to work together, but we're going to. It's good for both of us. Our companies. So let's do it right."

"The Jack Colton I remember was impulsive and liked life on the edge and always made spur-of-the-moment decisions," Serena said thoughtfully. "So when did you get so reasonable?"

"When I grew up," he blurted out, then glanced at Alli and softened his tone. "It happens. Even to those of us who fight it.

"And if that's how you saw me all those years ago," he added, "what made you think that I'd be a good husband?"

"Well, I guess I just hadn't grown up yet," Serena said quietly.

Four

When she and Alli walked into their penthouse apartment in Newport Beach, the first thing that came to Serena's mind was *Always have an OCD housekeeper.* It wasn't the first time she'd had that thought. Since hiring Sandy Hall when Alli was a newborn, Serena had had plenty of time to appreciate the woman. Serena's spacious apartment was always perfect and Sandy was always happy to watch Alli. At sixty, the housekeeper was active, opinionated and someone Serena could count on.

Alli took off the moment the door opened, racing for the kitchen, where she knew there would be cookies and milk waiting for her.

Serena thought about stopping her—after all, they'd just had ice cream—but one day of a sugar rush wouldn't hurt her. Walking into the main room, she dropped her purse on the plush rose-colored sectional and poured herself a glass of wine at the bar. She carried the glass with her out to the patio off the main living space and stood in the breeze, looking out at the ocean. No matter what mood she was in when she came home, that view was always enough to smooth her out. And, tonight, she really needed some serious smoothing.

Serena thought back to that one moment in the ice-cream shop, when she and Jack smiled together over Alli and there had been that…connection, which she supposed most parents shared when their kids were being cute or annoying or… But she and Jack weren't parents. They weren't together. So even considering that idea for a second was not going to happen. Ever again. One weak moment was enough to stiffen her spine.

She hoped.

"Thought you might like some cheese and crackers with that wine."

She turned and smiled at Sandy. The woman's natural red hair sported some gray, but her blue eyes sparkled with interest and curiosity. "You read my mind."

"Just one of my many talents," Sandy said and set the plate of snacks on the glass-topped table that was—of course—pristinely clean. "So, you went straight for the wine tonight. Rough day?"

"You could say that."

"Well, whatever it is, it's a new day tomorrow and anything can happen."

Basically, that was what Serena was worried about, but she wasn't going to admit it. Not even to herself. "Thanks, Sandy. And don't let Alli have too many cookies before dinner."

"Do I ever?"

As she walked off, clucking her tongue and shaking her head, Serena laughed. But then her thoughts turned back to Jack and the smile slid from her features. If he was only here for business, why did he insinuate himself into ice cream with her and Alli? Why was he being so kind to Alli, for that matter? Was he trying to use her daughter to get to her? Would he do that? She couldn't imagine the old Jack doing it, but as he pointed out, they'd both done a lot of changing over the last seven years. So, basically, she was left to wonder, *What's he up to?*

There was no way to know. Heck, even when they were a couple, Serena had had a hard time predicting his next moves. If she'd been able to, she never would have told him she loved him and set herself up for humiliation.

"No," she muttered, taking a seat at the table and reaching for a Brie-topped water cracker, "this time is going to be different, because I'm different.

I'm not the shy, quiet, trusting little soul I used to be, and in a way, I have him to thank for it."

If he hadn't run from her, she never would have fallen so easily for Robert, who had turned out to be a lying, cheating scumbag. But then she wouldn't have Alli, so, in a way, she owed Jack for her daughter, too. And Alli was worth anything.

Hell, fighting for Alli, standing up to Robert and getting him out of their lives was the first time she'd really felt sure of herself. Knowing that she was doing the right thing, she had been fearless in fighting for her daughter. That whole experience had tempered her. Made her grow. And in that weird way, she again had Jack to thank for it.

Though none of that meant she was willing to trust the man or his motives.

"Brace yourself, Jack," she muttered, then lifted her wine in a toast.

The following day, Jack was in his office, finalizing a few plans for the Colton Group's newest hotel.

He'd picked up a once-grand building in Florence, Italy, and was now busily transforming it into the jewel it would be in about six months. But there were plans to go over, adjustments to authorize and a contractor to keep in check. The man kept using the language barrier as an excuse for any "misreads" between him and Jack. But that wasn't going to fly for long. Jack had just finished arranging for his project manager—who spoke Italian—to fly over and set things back on track. If the Italian contractor couldn't do the job the way Jack wanted it done, then he would be replaced.

He hadn't built his company into one of the most exclusive hotel chains in the world only to ease off now.

Once he had the Italian situation handled, he opened his email and found one from Serena. Instantly, images of her filled his mind. From seven years ago and from last night. He never would have expected an ice-cream shop to be so filled with sexual tension, but Jack doubted he would ever see a chocolate-chip cone without thinking of Serena, slowly licking that frosty treat.

Frowning, he shifted position in his chair and focused on the email. Safer that way.

Jack—we need to work out the logistics for awarding airfare along with your hotel stays. And I need to know if you're going to be handling most of this with your own assistant or turning it over to me.
Serena

He sat back in the black leather chair, then swiveled it around to look out the window while his mind worked. Whether she knew it or not, that email from Serena had just given him the perfect excuse to back away from getting more entangled with both the Careys and the gala.

Jack didn't mind the grand giveaway he had planned. What he did mind was having to work with Serena to make it happen. Oh, he was pretty sure she was good at her job, because, family or not, Bennett wouldn't have her running her own department for the Carey Corporation if she wasn't.

But working with Serena was bound to bring back memories that were better off staying in the past. Not to mention kindling brand-new fires. Hell, it wasn't as if he'd been pining for her. Sure, he'd thought of her once or twice—how could he not? But he'd moved on a long time ago. Surely, the fact that Serena had been married, divorced and was now a single mom would prove that she wasn't holding on to the past, either. So why was he worried? Because of the damn buzz he felt every time he got close to her.

He couldn't afford to be distracted. Jack needed this to go well. He was putting a lot of faith into Serena and the Carey family fundraiser. If this went well, it would get him the kind of media attention you just couldn't buy.

"Second-guessing this whole giveaway?"

His assistant's voice cut into his thoughts and dragged Jack back to the present. He looked up at her and shook his head. "Oh, hell no, Karen. This giveaway is going to be hugely popular. The great press we get over this will more than compensate for any losses we swallow for the free stays."

Karen was fiftyish, happily married and the mother of five sons, only two of whom were still at home. She was ruthlessly organized, scrupulously honest and had a way of getting things done. She'd only been with him three weeks, but Jack had a feeling she was there to stay. Hell, he only wished he'd had her in England.

"I'll say it is," she said. "One week every month for a year? At any of the Colton Group hotels in the US or Europe?" She shook her head and gave a long sigh. "I might have to buy one of those tickets myself."

Jack laughed. "How about instead you set up an appointment for me with Serena Carey for tomorrow. I want to go over the plans for this whole—" He paused, thought about it and finally said, "I don't want to say 'raffle' because that sounds too small…"

"It does. But the prize certainly doesn't." Karen double-checked her notes, then lifted her gaze to his. "And the most important thing is that a lot of children will be helped by the money raised at the gala. The Careys have always supported children's causes, and thanks to you offering this spectacular prize, this year will be better than ever."

"Hope you're right." He picked up a stack of papers, set them to one side, then grabbed his cell phone. "Take care of that appointment, will you? I'm just calling Bennett to make sure we're all on the same page."

She nodded and left the room, but Jack didn't watch her go. Instead, he punched in Bennett's number, then turned to look out at the ocean. One of the perks of having his office right on the Pacific Coast Highway was the wide, sweeping view. The Pacific was so tame compared to the wild, raw beauty of the Atlantic. And yet the Pacific meant home. Hell, he'd grown up in the Colton house in Laguna Beach, with the sound of the waves lulling him to sleep at night.

California called to him and probably always would. And, yeah, he assured himself, it was *just* California calling to him.

"Jack." Bennett's voice on the line.

"Yeah." He shook his head, told himself to concentrate and said, "I wanted to let you know everything is set on my end. We've got Marketing handling the images of the Colton hotels—that's Europe and US—and I'll deliver them to Serena myself."

"Oh, she'll be thrilled."

"Oh, yeah." Jack remembered the moment he'd walked into her office and the expression on her face. "When I stopped by the auditions last night, she threw herself at me. It was embarrassing. I think she wept."

"Yeah, I remember." Bennett laughed out loud.

Jack's eyes rolled. "Look," he said, "there's nothing between your sister and me. Not anymore. Not for years. I didn't come back for a big reunion. It just worked out that way."

"Hey, none of my business what you two get up to," Bennett said quickly, and Jack could almost see him holding up both hands in a surrender move. "Trust me when I say I learned the hard way to butt out of my sisters' lives."

Jack kept his gaze fixed on the ocean but said, "There's nothing to butt into, but good to know."

"Nothing, huh?" Bennett asked. "And yet after the auditions, you and Serena took Alli for ice cream."

"You hear plenty, don't you?" He frowned at the phone.

"I always do," Bennett admitted. "Oh, and just so you know?"

"Yeah?"

"Whatever happens between you and my sister? That's between the two of you." He paused for a long moment, then said quietly, "But don't hurt Alli's heart. She's off-limits."

"Seriously?" Insulted, Jack scowled out the window at the clear, bright day. "That's what you think of me?"

"Didn't say that," Bennett told him. "It's just a warning. All I'm saying is, we all love that little girl, so don't plan on using her to get to Serena without pissing off every one of the Careys."

"I don't use *anyone*," Jack ground out. "Least of all, kids."

"Then there's no problem," Bennett countered easily. "Hey, had to say something, man. Won't risk Alli."

As the first sting of insult faded, Jack could see his friend's point and allowed himself to be appeased, nodding thoughtfully. All the man was doing was protecting his family. Was it any less than Jack had done when he confronted his father to protect his mother? "Yeah, I get it."

"Thanks."

"Sure." Jack paused for a moment, then suddenly asked, "You busy tonight?"

"Why?"

"Want to grab some dinner?" Hell, it had been a long time since he'd seen his friend. It was time now to rebuild that relationship as well as he'd rebuilt his hotels.

"Sure," Bennett said. "How about seven at the Carey restaurant?"

Jack laughed and shook his head. "There is more than just your restaurant in Orange County, you know."

"None are as good."

Still laughing, Jack agreed. "Fine. Can I get a good steak there?"

"Best steak in California."

"I'll hold you to that," Jack said, grinning. "See you then."

He hung up, then tucked his hands into his pockets and watched the steady, relentless slide of the sea toward the sand. He was back home. His friend was here. His life was here now. It was time to make that life everything he wanted it to be.

All he had to do was figure out how he was going to deal with Serena.

He had one idea that he thought might work, and it would put them on an equal footing.

A few days later, Jack had found his rhythm. California life was very different from being in London. And it wasn't just the weather. He threw open the French doors off his bedroom and stepped out onto the looks-like-oak floor to the railing.

Taking a sip of coffee, he told himself that putting a Keurig in his bedroom was the smartest move he'd made in years. Not having to wait for coffee made every morning just that much brighter. Like today. He stared out at the ocean and listened to the music of the waves sliding into shore. The sky was a deep clear blue that boasted fast-moving white clouds like sails across an endless sea.

"It's good to be back," he told himself and headed inside to get a jump on the day. The Colton Group was climbing to the number one spot in the hotel world and he wouldn't stop until it was all the way there. He couldn't afford distractions, not even one so tempting as Serena—though, damn, she *was* tempting.

Shaking his head, he focused on work, not the woman who was taking up too many of his thoughts lately. Nothing corporate this morning, he thought, already planning his trip to the Dana Point hotel. He wanted to check in with the decorators, make sure they were on schedule for the grand opening in two weeks.

Giving away free stays at his hotel meant he'd damn well be ready to welcome those guests to the kind of five-star treatment that would have them talking about their "win" for years.

He wore black jeans, black boots and a long-sleeved white dress shirt. He grabbed up a black jacket on his way to the stairs and slipped it on. When his cell rang, he reached into his pocket for it, checked the readout and smiled. His day had just gotten even better.

"Hello, Serena. Miss me?"

"Dream on," she quipped, and he laughed. He liked this more confident, slightly sassy Serena even more than he had liked her back when.

He hadn't contacted her in days. Nothing about the gala, the raffle, the prizes, nothing. He'd wanted her to call him, and it looked as though his patience was finally paying off.

"Okay, then what's this about?" He took the stairs, glancing around at the latest changes made to the Colton house.

Some things remained the same, of course. The stairs and banisters had been hand carved by craftsmen a hundred years ago. The floors were wide plank oak, fitted together by those same craftsmen with such precision there was never a stray squeak heard. The walls were still plaster— now painted a sort of dark sand—studded with rough-hewn beams. There were enough wide windows to make it seem as if the outside was inside, and the surrounding gardens and trees made for picture-perfect views from every angle.

There were antique jewel-toned rugs strewn across the floors like islands of color in a sea of honey, and the furniture had been built for comfort and relaxation. What surprised Jack most about moving back was how much he was enjoying being in this house again. He hadn't been able to sell it because, as he'd told Serena, it had been in the family for far too long.

And while he was in Europe, he'd had caretakers—his housekeeper and her husband, the head gardener, living in the guesthouse for the last seven years.

So now Jack was rambling alone in a house built for a huge family.

But it was, almost surprisingly, home.

"What's this about?" Serena repeated. "You do remember we're supposed to be working together to set up yours and Bennett's big idea?"

He grinned, hit the bottom of the stairs and headed for the double front doors. Also hand carved by some long-lost craftsman that Jack now awarded a silent nod of appreciation.

"Sure, I remember. I also recall you not being very interested in it."

"Interested or not, it's already being advertised on our website, so we need to move on this, Jack."

Amusement faded into annoyance. She hadn't wanted any part of this and now she was calling the shots? "Serena, I'm on my way to the Dana Point Colton hotel to check things out, make sure we're on schedule."

He walked out the front door, down the stone steps and onto the circular driveway. His BMW convertible was waiting for him, black paint and shining chrome glinting in the sunlight.

"Fine," Serena said. "I need a complete list of the hotels you're offering in this raffle."

"All of them," he pointed out as he opened the car door and slid inside. "I told you that already."

"I know you did, but strangely enough, telling Marketing that you're offering up *all of them* doesn't do a lot for the advertising. I'd like a complete list of the hotels, along with descriptions, pictures if possible…"

Jack laughed a little. "That's a lot of information."

"I think we can handle it," she said.

"Yeah, I bet you can." He fired up the engine and it became a low, throaty purr in the background. "Look. I'm on my way to the hotel now. Once that meeting's done, I'll come to you. What do you say to lunch?"

An ocean breeze ruffled his hair and he picked up a pair of sunglasses off the passenger seat and slid them on while he waited for Serena to speak. It didn't take long.

"I say we can work in the conference room more easily."

He'd expected that. Serena would no doubt do whatever she could to keep them from being alone together. But he wasn't going to let that happen. He wanted some time with her. Maybe more than *some*.

"Suppose we could, but I'll be hungry by then. We can get the work done, as well as eat."

There was another long moment or two of silence and he could almost see her thinking over her options. He kept quiet, waiting.

Finally, she spoke. "Fine. We'll meet for lunch. Where?"

Jack laughed again as he shoved the gearshift into first. "I haven't been in town for seven years, Serena. You choose."

"Right. Okay. La Ferrovia. An Italian place close to our offices."

"I'll find it." He gunned the engine again and said, "Two hours?"

"I'll be there."

When he hung up and steered the car down the long drive, Jack was smiling.

Twenty minutes later, Serena was still wondering how Jack had smooth talked her into lunch when she walked into a family fight in the conference room. Sighing, she was suddenly happy she'd agreed to meet Jack on neutral ground. She walked into the room, took a seat near Amanda and watched Bennett try to referee their parents' latest argument.

"You're spending too much time on this Summer Stars program," Martin Carey said to his wife. "Candy, you're never home anymore."

"I'm surprised you noticed," their mother said, "since you're rarely there yourself."

"But when I do come home, you're always there," he complained. "Until lately."

"Ah, like the faithful family dog, am I?" she countered, cocking her head to glare at her husband. "I run to greet you at the door, bring you your slippers—"

"I don't wear slippers—"

"Irrelevant," she snapped. "I'm not a dog, either, and I'm not going to sit in that big house—just me and the housekeeper—waiting for the precious moments when you deign to show up."

"Now, Candy, you know I've been meeting with clients."

"Yeah, Dad," Bennett said, "but I could have handled that."

Their father swiveled his head to shoot his oldest child the death stare. "I'm trying to help you out while you become accustomed to being in charge."

"And how can he do that," Candace asked, "if you never allow him to *be* in charge?"

"Of course he is," Martin argued. "I'm only helping."

"How long has this been going on?" Serena asked, leaning toward Amanda.

"Feels like forever," her sister said, "but in reality, the last ten minutes. Bennett's doing his best, but even he can't keep Dad quiet."

Sad but true, Serena thought. Once Martin Carey was fixated on something, nothing short of a nuclear blast would knock him off course. And Martin, though he kept claiming to want to retire…didn't. Their mother, Candace, had had big plans for Martin's retirement. She'd wanted the two of them to do everything they'd put off over the years because of the business and raising their kids. But Martin couldn't let go of the reins and it was driving Candace crazy.

"Dad," Bennett said, and Serena heard the tension and the fight for calm in his voice.

In the best of circumstances, Bennett wasn't the

most patient man on the planet. But having spent the last several months caught between their battling parents, he was hanging on by a thread.

"Why don't you and Mom go talk this out at home?" A reasonable tone that Serena almost wanted to congratulate him for.

"We have nothing to talk about," Candace said, lifting her chin and glaring at her husband. "Not until your father agrees to keep his promises."

Serena's chin hit her chest. Honestly, they'd all been suffering through the ongoing war between their parents. Well, all but their youngest brother, Justin, who managed to never be around when the sparks started flying. Serena had long been Justin's champion because she, too, had fought to make a life outside the family company. Though she'd changed her mind and joined the firm, that didn't mean she thought Justin should. Still, that being said, it would be nice if he were there once in a while to share the heat with his siblings.

"Now," Candace said, "we either continue with the meeting or we call it over."

"I vote meeting," Amanda said with a quick glance at the wall clock.

"Fine," Bennett surrendered. Momentarily, no doubt. "Dad?"

"I'm agreeable."

Candace snorted. The most inelegant sound Serena had ever heard come from her mother. Apparently, they'd *all* been pushed to the breaking point. Honestly, she felt for her mom. Candace wanted to enjoy some time with her husband. The fact that he was choosing his business over her couldn't be an easy thing to swallow.

But she could see things from her father's point of view, as well. He'd taken the Carey Corporation higher than anyone would have thought possible. Of course he would have a hard time walking away from that kind of success.

And it was really hard seeing everyone's position and sympathizing with both of them.

"Serena," Amanda said loudly, to cover any other comments, "why don't you start? Is the catering finalized?"

"Yes." Grateful to be on solid ground, and for the change in subject, Serena opened up her tablet, scrolled to the gala section and then down to catering. "I met with Margot three days ago—"

"And we were supposed to meet to discuss it," her mother said.

She lifted her gaze to Candace. "I've been busy."

"That's no excuse," her father said. "This is a family company and the *family* will make decisions. Your mother deserves better from you."

Candace rolled her eyes. "I don't need you to defend me, Martin."

"I was just trying to point out that Serena should keep her word."

"Everyone should," Candace muttered.

She spoke up quickly to keep her parents from devolving into another argument. "Fine. I'll bring you up to speed tonight, Mom," Serena said, hoping to keep this train on the track. "Margot has some great ideas for the menu, and we'll be having food stations set up throughout the pavilion."

"Will that be enough?" Bennett looked worried.

"No, but that's why we're going to have additional tents set up in the garden with more food stations out there." Serena flipped the tablet around to show them Margot's designs for the stations. "People will be able to wander in and out of the pavilion and not be deprived of food while they do it."

"Sounds great," Amanda said, and Serena gave her a grateful smile.

"What kind of food?" Martin asked.

"The easy-to-carry-around kind," Serena told him. "The gala never holds a sit-down dinner. It would be logistically impossible with as many guests as we're expecting. So there will be all different sorts of finger foods, along with the most amazing little pastries, and I promise you no one will leave hungry."

"Good point, dear," Candace threw in.

Serena would have appreciated that, but she knew her mother had said it mostly to irritate her father.

"There'll be four open bars," she continued and scrolled to the placement designs. "Two in the pavilion and two in the garden. No one will have to wait long for a drink, and servers will be moving through the crowd with appetizers and champagne all night."

Bennett nodded. "Sounds like it's coming together."

"Thanks." Serena almost rolled her eyes but somehow restrained herself. "I've got the flowers arranged, too." Back to her tablet, she found the workup the best local florist had drawn up. "There will be your standard—but beautiful—bouquets near the dais where we'll be announcing the winners of the raffles and where Bennett will welcome everyone to the gala. We'll have individual vases on each of the high tables and more scattered throughout the pavilion and out in the garden."

"Those look fantastic," Amanda said, then wondered aloud, "I wonder if Celeste would be interested in doing my wedding flowers…"

"Don't see why not," Serena told her. "That's a great idea, actually. I'll give you her number."

"Thanks. I'll call her when the meeting's over."

"Which it isn't," Bennett said, speaking loudly enough to carry over his sisters. "I'm sure we're all thrilled that Amanda's wedding will have pretty flowers, but could we stay on topic?"

"For God's sake, Bennett," Amanda snapped. "If you're upset because you've lost a stick, I know where it is."

"Funny," her brother said. "How about you tell

us about the Summer Sensation lineup instead of wedding plans?"

Glad to have the spotlight off her, Serena sat back and listened to her sister outline the troubles she was having with a few of their regular performers. Including the new contract that included steaks and Hasselback potatoes with spinach and Pepper Jack cheese.

"What are they trying to do?" Bennett demanded.

"Trying to work us without asking for more money."

"Well, I think it's very tacky," Candace put in. "And if I remember correctly," she mused, "their performance last year was less than stellar. Perhaps next summer we think about a replacement for them."

"Not a bad idea, Mom," Amanda said.

"You're not still going to be doing this in a year, are you, Candy?" Martin asked, clearly surprised.

Slowly, she turned her head to look at her husband. "Are you planning to still be *helping* Bennett?"

He scowled at her.

"Exactly," Candace said. Then continued with a rundown on the Summer Stars auditions. "I had no idea there were so many talented people out there. Some of them have just been…amazing. I think people are going to have a hard time deciding who to vote for."

"Maybe I should take a look at the website design," Martin said.

"No, you should not," Candace argued, and all three Carey siblings sighed and sat back as the war escalated again.

Honestly, Serena told herself, maybe she had dodged a bullet when Jack left her seven years ago. Watching her parents fight and argue like a couple of children was enough to tell her that even nearly forty years of marriage didn't necessarily mean flowers and balloons every day.

Of course, she'd learned that anyway, with Robert. Now she was standing on her own two feet and she liked it. No one to answer to but herself. No one to worry about making happy. No one to argue with her about how to raise Alli. And no man was going to get in the way of any of that.

Yep. Single was sounding really good. At least it was quieter.

"Has anyone heard from Justin?" Bennett's voice dropped into the room like a hammer blow and immediately got everyone's attention.

"I did," Candace said with one last glare at her husband. "Justin's in La Jolla on business, he said."

"Business?" Bennett asked. "What kind of business does he have in a beach town near San Diego?"

"You know very well that La Jolla is much more than a simple *beach town*."

True, Serena thought. The small town not only boasted some of the best coastline views in California, it was also home to amazing restaurants, gorgeous homes, museums and even sea caves that drew snorkelers from all over to explore their depths.

"Fine." Bennett gritted his teeth. "It's more than a beach town. Why is Justin there?"

"Well, I don't know," their mother answered. "I don't interrogate my children."

"Is that supposed to mean something?" Martin asked.

"Probably. Is the meeting finished?" Candace looked from one to the other of them before finally pinning Bennett with a flat gaze.

"God, yes," her son answered, and Serena felt bad for him. He was in charge with everyone but the parents, who were driving them all a little nuts.

"Enough for one day. Next week, we'll meet again to go over any last-minute needs for the gala." Bennett shook his head as if clearing it of anything that had happened during their meeting. "If anyone needs me, I'm heading out for the day to meet with a client."

"Which client?" their father asked.

"Oh, Martin," Candace said, disgusted.

"I'll race you to the door," Amanda whispered as their parents started arguing again. She got up and headed out.

Serena was right behind her.

Five

Jack knew the moment Serena walked into the restaurant. Not because the owners shouted out a greeting. Not because he heard her laugh with friends.

But because Jack could have sworn that the air electrified when she arrived.

The restaurant was an upscale neighborhood place where regulars were treated like family. The floors were pine planks, the walls were a soft red dotted with pictures of Italy, the owners' family and even a signed photo of Frank Sinatra—which let him know that the restaurant had been around for a long time. Judging by the scents wafting from the kitchen, he could guess why.

Serena came around the corner and he stood up as she approached. His heartbeat jumped into a jagged rhythm just watching her walk toward him. Every nerve in his body fired at the suspicious look in her eyes and his blood burned thick and hot as his gaze swept over her. She wore a short black skirt, those red heels he'd already admired and a navy blue silk shirt with a deep V-neckline. She had her blond wavy hair pulled up off her neck today in some sort of tail that looked both messy and tempting, and her blue eyes were locked on him.

"Hello, Jack."

"Serena." He nodded, then sat down again when she took the chair opposite him. "I like your choice of restaurant."

"You'll like it more after you eat."

When the server showed up, Serena said, "Hi, Barbara. I'll have my usual. And iced tea."

"Unsweetened. Got it." She looked at Jack. "Do you know what you want?"

Yes, he did. But Serena wasn't on the menu. Jack looked at her. "What's your usual?"

"Eggplant parmigiana."

He glanced at Barbara. "Make it two. But I'll have a beer."

"Be right up."

She walked away, and Serena braced her elbows on the table and said, "I don't see the files you were going to bring me."

He laughed as the suspicion in her eyes darkened. "It's a digital age, Serena." Reaching into his shirt pocket, he pulled out a USB key and handed it over. "It's all on there. The hotels, pictures of the suites, the surrounding areas, descriptions. If you need anything else, my assistant will get it for you."

She took the key, nodded, then lifted her black leather bag and tucked it inside. "Okay, thank you. But I have to say that we could have done a simple handoff at my office or a file transfer."

But then they wouldn't have been here, or they'd have been on her home turf. Advantage Serena. Here they were on even ground. Hopefully, advantage him.

"True, but if we had, we wouldn't be sitting in a restaurant that smells like heaven."

Her lips curved and everything in him wanted to reach across the table and touch her. Just... touch her. Every time that urge, that rush of heat, swamped him, Jack was surprised at the strength of it. Seeing her and being with her again had reawakened feelings he'd thought long dead—or at least comatose. He curled his fingers into his palms to keep from acting on that impulse.

"I swear I can gain weight just taking a deep breath in here."

"If you're fishing for a compliment, not necessary," he said, giving her a slow once-over that should have set her on fire. "You're even more gorgeous than you were seven years ago and that's saying something."

Her eyes went wide and surprised. "Thank you, I guess. But I'm not looking for a compliment."

"From anyone?" he asked, curious. "Or just from me?"

She smiled, took a sip of the water Barbara had set in front of them. Her gaze met his as she said quietly, "Just you."

"Ouch." Jack grinned in spite of the sting of that verbal slap. Then he clapped one hand to his chest. "Direct hit."

Her smile deepened. "You're trying to tell me you have a heart?"

"Oh, I have one," he assured her. He knew that because at the moment his heartbeat was galloping.

"You just don't use it."

"Ouch again." He studied her for a long minute and liked the way her gaze met his and never strayed. Tipping his head to one side, Jack silently compared this new confident, forceful Serena to the quiet, almost shy woman he had known so long ago. She'd changed a lot over the years. But then, so had he.

One thing that hadn't changed? His reaction to her. He hadn't wanted to rekindle a damn thing between them. And yet...

"I don't remember you being quite so outspoken."

She waited to respond until Barbara set her tea and his beer on the table and then left again. Taking a sip of that tea, she set it down and said, "I had to learn a lot of things over the last several years. I've learned to stand up for myself. To go after what I want. To do whatever is necessary to take care of Alli and myself." Her mouth curved briefly as she added, "Nothing stays the same. You should know that, Jack."

She licked her lips and everything in him tightened painfully.

"Oh, agreed." He picked up the frosty beer bottle, took a slow sip, hoping the icy liquid would put out the fire inside. It didn't. Then he studied the label as if looking for something important. "You've done well for yourself. And your daughter."

She gave him an almost regal nod.

"And I'm not saying I don't like the changes, either. I'm just…noticing."

"You don't have to like them, Jack."

He tipped his head to one side and watched her. "I do anyway."

Her lips twitched slowly, reluctantly. "Thank you."

"See?" he said. "We're getting along already."

"Uh-huh." She shook her head and he wished her hair were down so he could watch the heavy blond mass wave with the movement.

Hell, even he was surprised by his reactions to her. A single smile from her burned inside him, sending heat to every corner of his body. Memories awakened in his mind of Serena stretched across his bed. Serena laughing and spinning in a circle while the wind on the cliffs pushed at her hair and the sky blue dress she wore. Serena, lifting her face for a kiss and hooking her arms around his neck to hold on to him and draw him close.

Those memories brought a slow sizzle to his blood, but he had to let them go because this was not the same Serena. As she'd said, she'd changed. But he'd done a lot of changing over the years, too. He wasn't ruled by his hormones anymore. He'd learned to tuck desire away into a small corner of his mind, and he only let it out when he was sure he could control the situation.

Right now? He wasn't sure.

She changed the subject by asking, "So you said you were going to the Dana Point hotel this morning. How's it doing?"

Jack almost thanked her for getting his mind off her and back onto safe ground.

"Looks amazing," he admitted. "I'm not usually a fan of what the decorators come up with for the hotels." Shaking his head, he added, "We were renovating a hotel in Chelsea—outside London," he explained.

"Yes," she said, laughing. "I know where Chelsea is."

"Right. Sorry. Anyway, when I saw the designs from the *decorator*, it gave me cold chills. Lots of flowing white cloth and white rugs and white furniture and white quartz counters." He shivered in memory. "It was like falling into a marshmallow nightmare."

Serena grinned. "What were they thinking?"

"I don't know," he admitted, pausing for a swig of beer. "She said it was ethereal, meant to welcome guests into a cocoon of relaxation and warmth."

She laughed out loud and he found himself laughing with her.

"Oh, wow. I hope you didn't go with it."

"Please." His laughter slipped away as he said, "No. We went with another decorator who kept the dignity of the old building and gave it the upgrades it needed to become the most exclusive, sought-after hotel in the area. Check the USB key I gave you. You can see how it ended up."

"I will."

Nodding, he continued, warming to his theme. "There are way too many decorators out there who want to go with the *trendy* ideas, forgetting that trends come and go. Have to say, though, the one I hired for Dana Point nailed it. Somehow, she managed to pull together the beach feel, along with luxury, that really works."

"Sounds beautiful," she said.

"Really is. You should come see it." Suddenly, the thought of Serena at his hotel was very appealing. Of course, even more appealing was having her at his house. In his bed. Under him. Over him.

Hell, the fascination with her was deepening by the minute. His attraction to her was stronger than it had ever been and the craving for her was gnawing at him. The more time he spent with her, the more he wanted her. She was strong and he liked that. Sure of herself and it was damned intriguing. Not afraid to give as good as she got and he liked that, as well.

Plus, as he'd told her, she was even more beautiful than she had been seven years ago, and that was really saying something. When she pushed one hand through her hair, it was a sensuous movement that caught his eye and stopped his breath.

Jack's imagination was running wild with all kinds of ideas involving Serena. And the more he entertained those images, the harder it was to breathe past the need.

"You've got a weird look on your face," she said quietly. "What're you thinking?"

"Maybe you shouldn't ask questions you might not want to know the answer to," he said softly.

She only stared at him, a thoughtful expression on her face. "Well, that's vague enough."

"Let your imagination fill in the blanks."

"You sure about that?" she asked.

"Nervous?" he countered.

One corner of her mouth lifted. "Not a bit."

Yeah, he really liked this new Serena. A lot. Maybe *he* was the one who should be nervous.

When their lunch was served, they each got quiet for a few minutes until Jack broke the silence. "This is amazing."

She grinned. "It really is. Mandy and I come here for lunch a lot."

"I know why."

Nodding, Serena sipped at her tea and asked, "So how many hotels have you got listed on that USB key?"

"All of them."

"Uh-huh. All is how many, exactly?"

He smiled. "Thirty-five hotels worldwide and still growing."

Her eyebrows lifted. "Impressive. You've been busy the last seven years."

"I have." An understatement of epic proportions. Those first few years it had been a 24/7 proposition. Constantly working to rebuild a company his father had allowed to fall into ruin. By doing that, the old man had let Jack know that he hadn't given a flying damn how Jack and his mother would live. What they would do when the Colton Group crashed and burned. So Jack had worked his ass off to not only fix what had gone wrong, but to expand their holdings until the Colton Group demanded respect around the globe as it did now. And his mother's future was secure no matter how her second marriage worked out.

"Didn't the Colton Group have twenty hotels back then?"

"Yes. But like you said, things change if you want them to badly enough." He took another sip of beer. "I revamped the standing properties. They all needed a face-lift, so to speak. And once they were finished and profitable again, I spread out. Buying up hotels that had been left to rot and turning them into the kind of hotels that people dream about."

Serena watched him with surprise, and was that...admiration in her eyes?

"You turned it all around after the mess your father left behind. Like I said. Impressive."

He stiffened slightly. Jack didn't like knowing that others were aware of what his father had done to the family legacy. With his reckless disrespect for actual work, he'd allowed most of their hotels to fall into disrepair and their flagship hotel in London to become a shadow of what it had once been.

Now it was back, better than ever, and it was because Jack had given up everything in his life that wasn't work. Yeah, he'd run from Serena when she said she loved him. Not only because he hadn't been ready for anything that even resembled commitment or *forever*. But because he'd seen "love" up close and personal in his own damn family.

And what his father called love had left his mother in tears most days and their family business shattered. Love hadn't meant a damn thing to his father other than as a weapon he could use or a weakness to exploit.

So Jack had left, not just because he didn't believe in love, but because he had no idea what to do with love when it was offered to him. He had been convinced that staying with Serena then would have turned out badly for her, and he wouldn't do that to her.

And to be honest, he'd left because he knew that if he wanted to save his business, his company, he didn't have the time to devote to any woman.

Even Serena.

Things were different now. His company was as big and successful as—maybe even more than—the Carey Corporation. His mother was happy. His father was so far out of the picture he didn't even rate a mention.

And Serena was…different, too.

Somehow more intriguing, more attractive, more…dangerous to him than she'd ever been. And though Jack insisted that he had changed, too, *love* was still a foreign word to him. An emotion he wasn't sure he knew how to handle—or cherish.

But, he reminded himself sternly, no one was talking about love, were they?

Serena was watching him through narrowed eyes. "You can't possibly be offended because I know what your father did to the family business."

She'd obviously mistaken his silence for anger at the mention of his father's failures. She wasn't completely wrong, either. Though what he'd felt wasn't really anger. It was more shame for the kind of man his father had been. For the choices he'd made that endangered his family. For the fact that the old man hadn't cared about that, either.

No one liked to be reminded of their family's disasters. Hell, he'd been fighting against his father's miserable reputation for years.

"I'm not offended," he told her quietly, "but it's not like I enjoy remembering or knowing that everyone else knows. Would you like to be gossiped about?" he countered.

"Please." She waved that away and took another bite of her side of fettuccine. After she swallowed, she shook her head. "Whatever happens to the Carey family makes the news. Remember? My grandfather having that affair with the actress and my grandmother trying to run them down in Grandpa's prize Bentley outside the Hollywood Bowl?"

He snorted, both at the memory and at her easy acceptance of her family's very public foibles. "Oh, yeah, that's right. Your grandmother said her one regret was missing them when some stranger interfered and pushed the happy couple out of the way."

She nodded. "Gran wasn't the forgiving sort."

"I sense that." He thought he would have liked her.

Serena grinned at him as if she knew what he was thinking. "When it was all over, Gran had the Bentley squashed, placed in her front yard, and had the gardener plant roses around it."

He laughed out loud, imagining it.

Serena laughed, too. Then, shaking her head, she continued, "When my dad took over the company after Grandfather left with the actress—in *her* car, obviously—there was all kinds of public speculation about how he would fail because he wasn't as ruthless as my grandfather." She took a bite of the eggplant, and while she chewed, she thought about it some more. "My mother took out a full-page ad challenging the reporter to prove Dad wasn't ruthless—which seemed a weird tack to take—but he couldn't do it, so he apologized, in print."

"The women in your family are a little scary," Jack mused, enjoying her more and more.

"We are," she said, nodding solemnly. Then a brief bright smile destroyed the solemnity. "You should keep that in mind."

"Believe me when I say I will," he vowed.

"Good to know. Let's see," she mused, staring at the ceiling before looking at him again. "Oh, my divorce made for great reading when the newspapers and the internet actually printed a *list* of the skanky women my husband cheated on me with."

He winced as he imagined how humiliating that would have been for her. "That's cold."

"And then some," she agreed, then shrugged. "Of course, it made it much easier for my attorney to get me full custody of Alli and for Bennett to pay off Robert so I'd never have to deal with him again."

Nodding, he said, "That's good."

"Very good," she agreed and took a sip of tea. "The last big piece of gossip was when Justin flunked out of college. That was a biggie. Oh, so-called reporters *loved* the story of the black sheep of the Carey family failing."

Okay, she'd made her point. She knew all about bad press. Maybe even more than he did. And not once had the Carey family run and hidden from the gossips or the nosy reporters and the salacious tabloids. They just went on about their business and pretty much said the hell with them. But the Justin thing he didn't understand. "Why's that so big? Hell, a lot of people don't go to college and they do fine."

"Not in the Carey family." Serena gave a wistful

smile, then took a bite of her lunch. After a long moment, she added, "For my dad, Justin leaving college was the last straw. The fact that the news seemed to enjoy the downfall of one of us only made things worse. I think my dad's convinced that his youngest son is just a loser." Her gaze lifted to meet Jack's. "And he's not. It's only that Justin's not a books-and-schedules kind of guy."

"I get that," Jack said, with some sympathy. "I'm not, either. Going to college was like being sentenced to prison. Hell, I couldn't wait to get out."

She smiled, but it was small and brief. "You stayed, though. Graduated."

"I had to." He took a long pull on his beer and said, "You were right. My father nearly lost the whole company because he couldn't be bothered to give a damn." He thought about it for a moment and then told her more than he'd told anyone. "My mother lost her home and that did it for me. The old man didn't care what happened to us, so I had to. I had to make sure my mom was safe. That she'd never have to be worried about losing her home again."

"God, Jack," she said softly. "I had no idea it was that bad."

"Glad to hear it," he said with a half smile. "Good to know gossips didn't report everything. Anyway, I knew that if I was going to save the company, I'd need a degree in business. I got it. Sweat through those classes because I knew what was waiting on the other side. Seven years ago, dear old Dad finally disappeared, taking as much cash as he could with him. So I had to go back. Focus on the company. On saving what I could and reinventing everything else."

"I didn't know."

"And I didn't want to tell you," he admitted.

"I get that, but I still wish you had," Serena said.

"It wouldn't have made a difference, Serena." He looked at her, his gaze locked with hers. "I couldn't give you what you needed from me."

"Well." She sat back and kept her gaze fixed with his. "We'll never know for sure, will we?"

Before he could argue that point, she changed the subject—or rather, went back to the original one.

"Anyway, we were talking about Justin. And the truth is, Justin doesn't have that ambition that you had, pushing at him." She shrugged and pushed a bite of eggplant all over her plate. "I guess he just doesn't know what he wants for himself yet. Except he's made it pretty clear he does not want any part of the Carey Center."

Jack had been headed toward leading the Colton Group all his life, and he couldn't imagine doing anything else. But if he'd had three older siblings to compete against, who knew what he might have chosen? "Where is Justin these days?"

"Last I heard, La Jolla." Serena slid her plate to one side, clearly giving up on finishing the excellent meal. "He doesn't come to family meetings, avoids phone calls and practically moves through the family like a ghost. The only ones he really talks to at all are me and my mom…and lately, more Mom than me."

He heard the worry in her voice and wished he could ease it somehow. He didn't even question that impulse. "How's Bennett with all of this?"

She laughed wryly. "You know Bennett. He *is* rules and schedules. The man wouldn't know what to do with himself if someone told him to *wing it*."

Now Jack laughed at the very apt description of his friend. Hell, he hadn't enjoyed just *talking* to any woman like this in years. Actually, he thought, since the last time he'd seen *her*. Yet this new Serena was so much more than her younger self. She really had come into her own and he admired that.

Plus, there was something to be said for a woman whose family could be as screwed up as your own. What worried him was that he wanted to do a lot more than *talk* with Serena. Then she spoke up and he focused on the moment at hand.

"How's your mom loving Paris?"

He lifted one eyebrow. "And you know this how?"

"You to Bennett to me."

"Triple play," he mused, smiling. "Mom loves it. Her apartment—and I use that term loosely because it's more like a house on the third floor than an apartment. Anyway, it overlooks the Champs-Élysées, and every morning, so she tells me, she flings open the drapes and stares out at the most beautiful city in the world."

Serena gave him a wide smile. "So she's happy."

"She is." He inclined his head briefly and took one moment to remember the last time he'd spoken to his mother. She practically glowed these days and it was good to see. She'd had enough turmoil in her life, and it was long past time she had a chance to enjoy it with a man who realized just how wonderful she was. "And it's not just Paris making her happy. It's her new husband, John. I admit, when he first started coming around, I had him checked out."

"Of course you did," she said.

He just looked at her. "Thanks for understanding that."

"Jack, she's your mom, and I know how hard it was for her with your father."

She did. He hadn't kept it a secret from her when they were together. Serena had allowed him to be furious. To vent and shout his frustration at not being able to free his mother from the man making her life a misery.

"Yeah, it was bad. But her husband now?" Jack smiled just thinking about his stepfather. "The man's amazing. He makes her laugh. Takes her dancing, brings her flowers and enjoys the same long walks she always has. Thinks my mom is the best thing that ever happened to him and spends every day making sure she's happy."

"Fairy-tale ending," Serena mused. "The world needs more of those."

"Yeah. I guess maybe it does." Which was an odd thing for him to think, much less say. But looking into Serena's sky blue eyes made a man's mind a little...off balance.

More people were trickling into the restaurant and the waitstaff was bustling. As an employer, Jack was impressed. As a man enjoying a semi-private lunch, he was irritated at the addition of so many more patrons.

"So we're all caught up on personal stuff," she said. "How about we talk business?"

"Oh, I think there's plenty more to talk about before we have to resort to business." Although keeping things on a personal level was getting harder as the restaurant filled up.

"Resort to?" she echoed. "I thought you and Bennett were two of a kind. All business all the time."

"Most of the time." His gaze locked on hers.

"But I can take an afternoon off when I'm sitting opposite a beautiful woman."

She laughed and he realized that he'd missed the sound of her laughter. It wasn't shy or quiet or hesitant—not even when she herself had been. When Serena Carey found something funny, she wasn't afraid to show it. Most of the women he'd known over the last several years had that quiet, simpering laugh that always seemed so fake. Another reason he hadn't really been able to forget Serena. She was real.

"Come on, Jack," she finally said when her laughter died and she'd taken a sip of tea. "Empty compliments are too handy. Too easy."

"Why do you assume they're empty?" he wondered. Were the men around here so stupid they didn't see her for what she was?

She took a breath and sighed it out. "Because men aren't lining up to talk to me. Because I have a mirror. Because you always did have way too much charm."

"Thanks for that, anyway." He paused. "I think."

She grinned. "Let's just keep this from going any deeper into the personal zone."

"Don't know if I can," he admitted ruefully. "And that's a surprise to me, too."

Her eyes narrowed on him, and Jack wondered why she was almost *more* attractive when she was being suspicious. What did that say about him? he wondered.

Barbara dropped off the bill, then went away to check other tables.

"You'll just have to try," Serena said and gathered up her purse. Digging into the bag, she came up with her wallet, and Jack stopped her.

"Lunch is on me."

She stopped. "I don't think so. It's not a date, Jack. It's a business meeting."

"You want it to be a date?" Did he?

"I didn't say that," Serena corrected him. "And no. I told you, we're keeping things businesslike between us."

"Right." He reached for his wallet, took out a card and laid it on top of the check. "Well then, let's split it."

"Fine." She got her wallet out.

"No," he said, holding out one hand to stop her. "Not what I meant. I buy this lunch. You pick up the tab on our first date."

She laughed again. "That's not going to happen."

Suddenly, he was determined to get that date with her. Seven years ago, it had been easy. She'd made no secret of how she felt about him. Back then, she'd been as eager as he to be alone together. Nights with Serena had been long and filled with a passion that he'd never found with anyone else.

But as much as he wanted her, should he really open that door again?

Hell yes, a voice in his mind whispered. *Push it open if you have to.*

Being around Serena again had awakened something in him that he'd thought was dead and buried. And Jack wouldn't be satisfied until he'd had another night with her.

Because he had to know. Had to discover if the connection they'd shared so long ago still burned between them. Had to know if this newer, more confident Serena was even more alluring in bed than she had been years before.

He'd done what he had to. Gone away. Built his business. Took care of his mom. Now he was back and Serena was here and there was…something worth exploring. Where it might lead, he didn't know and, at the moment, didn't give a flying damn.

All he knew was he had to have her.

"You remember how much I like a challenge, don't you?"

"Yes, I do." She took a breath, shook her head and said, "I'm not a prize at a carnival, Jack. I'm not something you win. I'm not your latest challenge and I'm not playing games with you."

"Neither am I." Except for a few specific games that were only played in a bedroom. Those he could get behind.

"Good. Then we're on the same page."

"Not likely," he said, because *his* page had her naked and sprawled across his bed wearing nothing but moonlight. That image put a smile on his face that Serena noticed.

"What? Why are you smiling?"

He signed the check when Barbara brought it back, then tucked his card back into his wallet. "Remind me of this moment someday and I'll tell you."

"You have to be vague?"

"Don't have to, no."

"So you just enjoy being an irritation?"

He grinned. "Turns out…yeah."

"Fine." She stood up, slung her bag over her shoulder and said, "I'll go over the list with my assistant, and if I have any questions, I'll call you."

"Looking forward to it."

"Call you about *business*, Jack."

"For now," he said. When she turned and walked away, Jack watched her go, just to appreciate the view. "She always did have a great butt," he whispered.

Six

"The hotels are amazing," Serena told her sister later that afternoon.

She hated that. Hated that Jack had done so well and was now here to make sure she knew all about it. Hated that she'd had such a good time at lunch and *really* hated that he could make her body buzz and burn with that damned slow smile of his.

In Amanda's office, Serena paced like a prisoner counting off the steps of her sentence.

"He didn't have to meet me with the information," she muttered. "Why did he insist on meeting me?"

"Well—" Amanda said.

"Oh, no, he couldn't drop the list off at the office or email it. No, it has to be lunch." Words tumbled from her, one after the other until they were just a stream of consciousness she couldn't rein in and didn't bother to control. "And then he treats it like it's a date. I never said it was a date. Business. That's it. Period."

"What—"

As if Amanda hadn't spoken at all, Serena kept babbling. Worse, she *knew* she was babbling and couldn't stop. "*Then* he says he'll buy lunch and I can pay for the meal on our first date." Shaking her head, she whirled around, stabbed a finger at her sister and said, "Our first date was seven years ago. Right?"

"Right, but—"

"Seven years ago! So how can we have a first date? We can't. That's how." First date. The man had said that on purpose just to get a rise out of her, and here she was, doing exactly as he'd planned. "And I don't want a date with him, no matter what number it is."

"Yeah, you do." Amanda managed to push out an entire sentence this time, and it was enough to stop the steady stream of complaints.

"What?"

Amanda laughed shortly. "Oh, you heard me. Don't pretend you're suddenly deaf." She shook her head and muttered, "Though I may be after listening to that blistering rant."

"Funny." Serena huffed out a breath and set both hands on her hips. "Okay, fine. I heard you. I just don't believe you. How could you even suggest that?"

"Well, for heaven's sake, Serena, look at yourself." Amanda waved a hand in her direction. "Pacing and muttering like a bad actress in an old melodrama. All that's missing is you clutching a string of pearls."

"Thanks very much." She'd have been insulted if it weren't true. Though she didn't want to admit that, obviously.

Still laughing, Amanda stood up, walked to the coffee bar on one wall of her office and poured herself a cup. "Do you want one? No. Never mind. You're wound tight enough."

"I am not tightly wound, and yes, thanks," Serena said. "Coffee."

Amanda shrugged and poured. "The point is, Jack asking you out on a date—"

"He didn't ask," Serena interrupted. "He proclaimed."

"The horror!" Amanda laughed. "Release the pearls, sweetie."

"Oh, stop it."

"The point is," Amanda repeated, a little louder this time, "you want the date."

"I do not. I—" She stopped talking, sipped at her coffee and quietly fumed at the fact that her sister knew her so well.

"Yeah, you do. Basically, you want *him*. You always have."

Oh, God, her sister had a point. Back in the day, all it had taken was a single look from Jack to turn Serena into a puddle of desire. It was a little lowering to admit that she was still in the same boat when it came to him.

But was she really? Seven years ago, she'd been so wrapped up in Jack she hadn't really thought beyond him. Now she could admit she wanted him while not putting her life on hold to dance attendance on the man. Didn't that make her sort of in charge now? Besides, she hadn't wanted to want him, but it seemed that desire didn't respond to her commands. It just demanded what it wanted. And it wanted Jack.

"Fine. I used to want him." Damned if she'd admit she still did. "But things are different now. I'm older. Smarter. I have a child. And the stretch marks to prove it," she added in a dark mutter.

"None of which makes you impervious to the need for sex." Amanda smiled to herself. "Especially great sex."

"This is not helping." She drank her coffee and burned her throat all the way down.

"It's the only thing that will," Amanda told her

as Serena started pacing again. "Go out with him. Go home with him. Have crazy naked sex with him." She shrugged. "Then get over it and move the hell on already."

Serena stopped dead and stared at her sister. "Now you're talking about you and Henry. This isn't about you. This is *me*."

"Pardon me for letting my mind drift a little," Amanda said. "But are you actually trying to tell me you *didn't* have great sex with Jack?"

Erotic images rolled through Serena's mind with a clarity that stole her breath. It was as if every night she and Jack had spent together was now rising up in her mind to torture her with her own memories. His touch. His taste. The way his hands felt on her skin. The look in his eyes as his body entered hers. She remembered it all in vivid detail.

And sometimes in her dreams it was as if she relived it all, only to wake up aching. So, yeah. *Great* didn't begin to describe what she'd had with Jack.

Their connection had been so strong, the chemistry between them so overwhelming that she'd simply assumed they would be together forever. That he felt what she did. But she'd been wrong then, and this time around, she couldn't afford to make the same mistake. She had Alli to think about now. It wasn't only her own heart on the line.

But why even consider that? They weren't talking about hearts and love and forever. Like Mandy had just pointed out, they were talking about great sex and then moving on, right? Could she do it? Could she keep her heart out of the mix entirely and simply use him as he'd once used her? Could she be the one to walk away this time?

"I see you thinking," Amanda mused with a smile curving her lips. "Is that a good sign?"

"Maybe," Serena admitted. Now that Amanda had planted the seed in her mind, she couldn't stop considering it. From all perspectives, of course. It wasn't as if she'd go into anything blind and trusting. Not again.

She stared across the room where afternoon sunlight was washing through the tinted glass. Dust motes danced in the air as Amanda's words rolled through her mind.

"Now you're thinking too much. Stop it!"

Amanda's sharp order shook her out of her thoughts. "You started it."

"I didn't mean for you to run home and make a pro-and-con list, for God's sake." Setting her coffee cup down on the mahogany bar with a sharp click, Amanda put both hands at her hips. "You're my big sister, Serena, but sometimes I swear I feel ages older than you."

"Thank you very much." She didn't care for being told that she was acting like a child. Especially when it was true. "I have more to consider than you did, Mandy, when you started things up with Henry again. There's Alli to think about, remember?"

"Um, not likely to forget my gorgeous niece, but she's not a part of this, right?"

"Exactly. And I want to keep it that way."

"And you can." She sighed. "Neither of you is looking for anything permanent, right?"

"As far as I'm concerned," Serena agreed, "absolutely."

"Then what's the problem?" Amanda threw both hands high. "Go get him, and once you've had him, lose him."

"You make it sound so easy."

"It's only hard if you want it to be," Amanda said.

"And you come by all this wisdom how?"

"Trial and error. Plenty of error." Moving closer, Amanda gave her a hard, tight hug, then stepped back. "God knows I made lots of mistakes where Henry's concerned. And I'm trying to help you avoid doing the same thing.

"It's hard for me to see you getting all wound up over Jack being here. If you don't like how things are, then change them. Take control of the situation, Serena. Don't let him dictate how you feel."

Her words rattled around in Serena's brain for several long moments before she was forced to admit that Amanda was right. She had been allowing Jack to steer this relationship—or whatever it was. He showed up, she was nervous. Or angry. Or excited. Or all of those emotions at once. Why?

She'd learned her lesson about Jack a long time ago, so why was she still behaving as if she hadn't? She'd done a lot of changing over the years—because *she* had decided it would be so. Was this any different?

Heck, couldn't she look at this as her last big test? The final exam on getting over Jack and moving on with a life that was turning out pretty great?

"You know what? You're right."

Amanda blinked, then grinned. "Wow. Where's a recorder when you need one? I'd love to be able to play you saying that to me over and over again."

Serena gave her sister a rueful smile. "Does Henry really know what he's getting into?"

"He does and he's lucky to have me."

"That's very true," she said and reached out to hug her sister. Then Serena took a deep breath, steadied herself and said, "I'm going to do it. I'm going to arrange a date, go back with him to his house and have my way with him."

Amanda laughed. "You sound like a Victorian heroine. You can use the word *sex*, you know."

Serena shot her a sidelong glance. "I'm not going to settle for using the word."

The following day, Jack stopped by the Carey corporate offices with one destination in mind.

He hadn't been able to get Serena out of his mind since their lunch date. All night, he'd been haunted by memories that were so stark, so real, that he'd actually been reaching for her when he woke up that morning.

He didn't like being twisted around by his own dreams and it was time to put a stop to it. Jack walked to Serena's office, nodded at her assistant, then strolled through the door and into her office. He liked catching her off guard. He'd expected to see a jolt of surprise in her eyes, but he hadn't expected…speculation.

"Jack." She gave him a smile that was both seductive and secretive. Now he was intrigued.

"Serena. I wanted to go over a few last-minute changes to the hotel lineup."

"What changes?" Serena sat back in her desk chair and stared at him. She was wearing a lemon yellow silk shirt with a wide collar that skimmed over her shoulders. Her honey-blond hair fell in soft waves that made him want to spear his fingers through it.

She looked beautiful. Damn it.

"We're sending the program to the printer this afternoon."

"Then I'm just in time," he said, dipping one hand into his pocket and coming up with a USB key. He walked closer, handed her the black key and said, "Not a big deal. I'm just adding one more hotel to the mix."

She glanced at the key, then up at him. "Which hotel?"

"It's my newest place in Santorini. The infinity pool was finished ahead of schedule, so we're ready to go there." Actually, that hotel was a gem. One of his favorites and it had been a damn wreck when he bought it just six months before. Now it sat on top of a cliff with a view that people would kill for. "I put the latest pictures on that key. Even I have to say they're impressive as hell."

"Okay. I'll get them to our art director and he'll include them when he sends everything to the printer."

"Great." He wandered over to the window, stared out at the view of the greenbelt and more office buildings, and told himself he'd made the right call setting his headquarters in Newport Beach. After a moment, he looked back over his shoulder at her. "Do any more thinking about that *date* we talked about yesterday?"

"Actually," she said, standing to face him, "I have."

He turned toward her. "And?"

"And what about tonight?"

Now it was his turn to shoot her a suspicious stare. "You want to go out with me tonight."

She eased one hip against the corner of her desk, and his gaze swept over her from that yellow silk shirt to the short white skirt and the beige heels that made her legs look amazing. His eyes lifted to hers and he saw that glint of speculation again. He wasn't sure what to make of this change of heart she was showing, but he'd be a fool to turn down the opportunity to get her alone.

"Don't tell me you've changed your mind and now you're not interested," she said, one corner of her mouth tipping up into a tease of a smile.

"Didn't say that." He tucked his hands into his pockets. "I am a little curious what changed for you. All of a sudden you *want* a date, when just yesterday you said it would never happen?"

She shrugged. "A woman's prerogative?"

"Really?" He snorted. "An old cliché?"

"What's the matter, Jack? Don't you trust me?"

"Sure, I do," he said, though even to himself he sounded less than convincing.

"Great." Her smile was wide and bright. "Then we're on," she said and pushed away from the desk.

She leaned over to pick up the USB key and Jack had a second or two to enjoy the view before she straightened up and faced him again. "I'll just get this down to Marketing. Was there anything else you needed, Jack?"

He couldn't take his eyes off her, and that should have sent alarm bells ringing in his head, but it didn't. Instead, all he could see were her big blue eyes, that mass of blond hair and those gorgeous long legs. Hell, he'd come here today hoping to charm her into going out with him, and now she was. Why wasn't he happy about that?

"We are on for tonight, aren't we?" she asked, bringing him up out of his thoughts.

"Yeah." He nodded. "Of course. I'll pick you up—"

"That's all right." She interrupted him with another smile, bright and shining. "I'll come to you. See you at Colton house at seven?"

"That works."

"Great," she said and walked to the door. At the threshold, she paused and looked back at him. "See you then."

And she was gone.

Alone, Jack stood in her office watching the door through which she'd disappeared, trying to figure out just where he'd lost control of the situation. She was being too damned cheerful. Eager, almost. What was happening? What was she up to?

"Hell, why do you care?" he asked himself and listened to his own voice break the silence in the room. Whatever the reason she'd agreed to go out with him, he was going to be grateful for it. He'd wanted her all to himself and he was going to get her. Why should it matter how it happened, as long as it did?

He'd worry about the whys of the situation some other time. Right now, he was going to enjoy the ride, wherever it took him.

* * *

Serena looked great and she knew it.

Her hair was loose and waving around her shoulders. She wore a black figure-hugging dress with a deeply square neckline and slim shoulder straps. Black heels completed the outfit, and the tiny black bag hanging off her shoulder held everything she might need.

She pulled up in front of the house, and when she got out of her car, she took a moment to stare up at the place she'd once spent more time in than her own home. Wood weathered by the sun and the ocean air, glass gleaming in the last rays of the setting sun, it looked as if it had simply grown out of the ground on its own. Surrounded by trees and flowering shrubs, it boasted manicured lawns and neatly tended flower beds where brightly colored blooms bobbed and swayed in the breeze.

Serena took a deep breath, dragging in the scent of the ocean and cooling her blood with the chill in the air. Since she'd decided her course of action only the day before, Serena had been sure she was doing the right thing. Have sex with Jack to get him out of her system once and for all. Sounded simple enough, but she'd learned long ago that nothing was simple when it came to Jack Colton.

Still, this time *she* was in charge. She was making the moves and deciding how things would go. This time, she wouldn't be blindsided by love because love wasn't going to be a part of the equation. This was about taking control. This was about feeding the hunger inside her and then, finally, really moving on.

Yet in spite of everything, including that mental pep talk, now nerves began to skitter through her body. Irritated, she squashed that feeling down and told herself to get on with it. Walking up to the wide double doors, she eyed the heavy pewter knocker before simply ringing a doorbell that released chimes inside the house.

She swung her hair back, and smiled when Jack opened the door. His gaze swept over her and she felt that look as if he'd touched her. Serena shivered a little, and he said, "Are you cold?"

"Not even a little," she answered and walked past him into the house.

A few steps into the entryway, she turned to face him. He looked…delectable. His dark hair a little unruly, his blue eyes locked on her and simmering with a banked heat that she felt echoing inside her. He wore a black long-sleeved shirt, black slacks and gleaming black shoes. He looked dangerous and she had reason to know he could be.

Tonight, she didn't care.

"You look amazing," he murmured and closed the door with a careless push.

"Thank you," she said and did a slow turn, enjoying the fire in his eyes when he looked at her.

"Yeah. Amazing," he repeated, his voice even lower than it had been. "So, where are we going on this date?"

Here it was, she thought. What she'd come here for. All she needed was the courage to go through with it. And looking into his eyes was enough to spur her on. Above those double doors, there was a stained glass arched window, and as the late evening sun poured through the panes, it became slants of jewel-toned lights that gave off a magical air.

Taking one slow step after another, she walked toward him and kept her gaze fixed to his every movement. She saw the flare of heat. The glint of desire, and it kindled the burning embers inside her into a bonfire ready to rage. Nerves disappeared and hunger rose up, rich and thick, inside her. *In charge*, she reminded herself. This time, it was all up to her. "I was thinking that maybe we'd stay here."

"Is that right?"

She laid one hand on his chest and felt the hard hammer of his heartbeat beneath her palm. His eyes flashed. His jaw tightened and his eyes when he looked at her darkened until they became the color of a storm at sea.

"I don't want to go out," she whispered.

"What do you want?" he asked, catching her hand with his and holding her palm to his chest.

Serena tipped her head back until she was looking directly into his eyes, and then she said only, "You, Jack. I want you."

He wrapped one arm around her waist and pulled her tight against him. She felt his erection pressing into her and she knew he wanted her as much as she did him. God, it had been so long since she'd been held. Kissed.

Curling her fingers into the neck of his shirt, Serena pulled Jack's head down to hers and kissed him. Softly at first, almost tentatively. But it took only a second or two for her to dive into that kiss. Her lips opened to him, and when his tongue swept into her mouth, her breath left her body in a rush.

He let go of her hand to wrap both arms around her, holding her to him with arms as hard and tight as iron bands, and still it wasn't close enough. She wanted more. *Needed* more. The kiss deepened further until she couldn't breathe at all and didn't care.

She felt his hand slide up her back to the zipper at the top of her dress, and when he tugged at it, she smiled against his mouth. He pulled on that tiny metal tab until the edges of her dress fell open and he could stroke her bare skin with his palm. Tearing her mouth from his, Serena let her head fall back on a sigh of pleasure.

His touch was the same, she thought. Gentle. Strong. Powerful.

Overwhelming.

"It's a good date so far," he murmured and dipped his head to kiss the base of her throat.

"Best one ever," she said on a sigh and cocked her head to give him easier access.

While he nibbled, she slid her hands up his chest to undo the buttons of his shirt. Once his shirt hung open, she skimmed her palms over his skin, loving the feel of those hard sculpted muscles beneath her hands.

"Believe it or not," he said, lifting his head to look down into her eyes, "I'm going to have to make a drugstore run. I'm not exactly prepared for this…*date*."

Serena smiled up into his eyes, then shrugged her purse strap down into her hand. Lifting the small bag high enough for him to glance at it, Serena said, "I've got you covered. Didn't want to take any chances, so I brought condoms."

"Damn, woman." He grinned at her. "You have a knack for planning every detail of a hell of a date."

"I'm very organized."

"And that's extremely sexy."

"Glad you think so," she quipped, then hooked her arms behind his neck. "So what do you say, Jack? Shall we get this date started?"

In answer, Jack bent down, caught her on his shoulder and then headed for the stairs. "Trust me on this, Serena," he said. "We've already started. And we've got all night to finish."

Seven

Serena felt a thrill sweep through her as Jack took the long winding staircase at a lope with her over his shoulder. She grinned as she slid her hands up and down his back, feeling his muscles bunch and release with his every movement.

Her insides quivered in anticipation and she pushed all thought aside in favor of simply *feeling* what was happening at the moment. She hadn't done that in years and it was…liberating.

"Still with me?" he asked.

"Absolutely."

"Good to know." At the top of the stairs, he took a right and headed down the long hallway. The pictures and photos on the walls were nothing but a hazy blur in the dim light and she didn't care. She wasn't there for a tour, after all. She knew this house. And knew Jack was taking her to his bedroom. That was all she cared about.

Once inside, he kicked the door shut, crossed to the bed and then flipped her over his shoulder to land on the wide mattress. A burst of laughter shot from Serena's throat as she bounced. "That was a smooth move."

He grinned as he took off his shirt. "You want smooth? Baby, I'll give you smooth."

"Give me everything," she countered.

He paused a long moment, looking down at her. "You want to tell me what brought this on?"

Serena stared at him, relishing the moment and the gleam in his eyes. She gave him a smile and asked, "Does it matter?"

He thought about it for a moment, then shook his head. "Not now it doesn't."

He undressed so quickly Serena didn't even get a brief glimpse of the room they were in. All she knew was that the king-size bed beneath her was soft and the man now looming over her was hard— in all the right places.

Jack lifted her foot and slipped off her high heel, then did the same for the other. His thumbs rubbed her insteps and had Serena sighing. "That's amazing."

"Just getting started," he promised.

He dropped her foot and reached out to her. When Serena laid her hand in his, he pulled her to her feet and she took a breath, hoping to steady the jolting beat of her heart. But how could it steady when she was so close to him? When she could feel the tension in his body mounting as her own was?

"Too many clothes," he murmured and finished dragging that zipper down the length of her back. When it was free, he pushed the shoulder straps off and down her arms until her perfect little black dress pooled at her feet.

His eyes widened slightly and she saw fire burning in those dark blue depths. The strapless black lace bra she wore with the matching black thong had done exactly what she'd hoped they would.

"You're full of surprises, aren't you?" His voice was a low murmur.

"I'm glad you like them," she said.

"Oh, *like* isn't nearly strong enough of a word."

She gave him a slow, satisfied smile, then reached to the front clasp of her bra and undid it.

"You're killing me here, Serena." He took a big gulp of air, then covered her breasts with his hands. At the first electrifying touch, Serena gasped and held her hands over his, capturing the closeness and holding on to it for as long as she could.

His thumbs moved over her nipples until a moan slid from her throat. And the sound fired something in Jack that had him tipping her back onto the bed and levering himself over her.

"Whatever brought you here tonight," he said, "I'm glad of it."

"Me, too." She reached up and pulled his face to hers. She kissed him hard, fast, deep, and it wasn't enough. She was a little afraid it never would be.

He broke the kiss and caught her gaze as he hooked his fingers in the slim elastic band of her thong. He pulled it off and down her legs, then cupped her center in the palm of his hand.

"Jack…" She lifted her hips into his touch.

"Just let me have you."

She met his gaze and said softly, "Yes. And I'll have you."

"That's a deal." He kissed her briefly, then slid down the length of her body until he was kneeling on the floor beside the bed. Then he took hold of her legs and pulled her toward him.

Serena's breath caught as she realized what he was planning. The cool silk of the navy blue comforter beneath her was a counterpoint to the heat engulfing her. Every sensation seemed to drop on her at once and tangle together.

The feel of his hands on her legs. The smooth slide of the comforter. The chill in the air. And then his mouth on her core.

Serena jolted in his grasp, but his big hands only tightened on her thighs, pinning her in place.

Jack's lips and tongue worked her body into a frenzy that had her mind spinning off into oblivion. She twisted and writhed against him as if she were trying to get away, and that couldn't have been further from the truth.

It had been so long since she'd felt anything like this. So long since she'd allowed herself to simply *be* in the moment.

Serena's thoughts came and went, and she was good with that. There was no time for thoughts when Jack was making her feel so much. Absolutely nothing mattered right now, except what Jack was doing to her. What he was making her feel.

His tongue licked and stroked at her core until she thought she might simply shatter. Serena groaned as he took her higher and higher. She didn't want it to end, but she knew she couldn't hold off much longer. If it were in her power, she would have kept him right where he was, doing magical things to her body forever.

But she couldn't wait. Couldn't keep from feeling the crash of relief hurtling toward her.

So she reached down, threaded her fingers through his hair and held his mouth to her as her body exploded. Again and again, the waves of release washed over her as she cried out his name on a shriek of pleasure that rocked her to her bones.

Struggling for breath, Serena trembled helplessly until Jack came to her, wrapped his arms around her and kissed her until what was left of her mind completely emptied. She lost herself in him as her body immediately rebounded from completion to need in a heartbeat. He cupped her face in his palms and devoured her. It was the only word that could describe how she felt under the onslaught of emotions he was bringing down on her.

When he broke the kiss, she blinked up at him, dazed and confused.

"Your purse. Where is it?"

Frowning, completely befuddled, she asked, "Purse? What?"

"Condoms, Serena," he muttered thickly. "In your purse. Condoms."

"Yes, yes." She shook her head and tried to think. "Dropped it. When you carried me."

"Damn it," he muttered and reeled off the bed. "Oh. It's here. Never mind. Thanks for not dropping it downstairs."

A short laugh shot from her. "You're welcome."

She watched him open her bag, grab the box of condoms and then toss the purse to one side. In a second or two, he had a condom out and sheathed himself.

Serena shifted restlessly, the need already clawing at her again. "Hurry up," she muttered.

He grinned at her. "Don't remember you being so impatient before."

"I don't remember you taking your time, either. Besides, I'm older now," she quipped. "I have less time to waste."

"Right there with you," he said and joined her on the bed again.

In one swift, hard thrust, he pushed his body into hers and she yelped at the invasion. But in the next second, she lifted her legs, wrapped them around his hips and rocked up to meet and match his rhythm. It was easy between them, like a physical memory. Just like seven years before, they moved together as if they were dancing. Each of them reacted to the other as if they were linked mentally, as well as physically.

She stared up into his eyes and couldn't look away from the racing flood of emotions darting across his features. Being with him again was more than she had thought it would be. It was touching her more deeply. Making her feel things she had deliberately let die seven years before. He was at once the same as he had been then and so much more.

A small corner of her mind told her she should be worried about the effect he was having on her, but instead Serena's body hummed with eager anticipation. Dismissing everything but what she was experiencing at the moment, Serena gave herself over to the raging physical need swamping her. She ran her hands up and down Jack's back, scraping her nails along his skin as if marking her territory.

Which was a ridiculous thought, so she pushed it aside instantly.

"Stop thinking, Serena," he whispered. "Just be with me."

"I am with you," she insisted and cupped his face with her hands. "Only with you."

He dipped his head to kiss her, and as he did, her body began that rocket climb to a peak she ached for. She moved with him, against him, and pleaded brokenly for what she needed.

"Let go, Serena," he said, his voice a low hush in her ear.

"No." She shook her head vehemently. "No. Come with me. We go together."

"Then hold on to me, baby, and we'll make that jump."

In just a few minutes, they did. He shouted her name, held her tightly, and when they fell, Serena locked herself around Jack, holding on to him as if determined to never let him go.

Jack rolled to one side, but kept Serena close, tucking her head against his chest as he lay there staring at the ceiling. His breath crashed in and out of his lungs and he felt both energized and relaxed. Mostly, though, he was stunned. When she'd agreed to a date, he'd expected dinner and a few hours of talking and then maybe charming her into his bed.

Serena had flipped all of that upside down and he was still having a hard time believing it. This was so far from the Serena he'd once known he didn't know what to do with it—beyond enjoy the turnaround. Turning his head to look down at her, he finally asked, "Not that I'm complaining...but what the hell happened here, Serena?"

He felt rather than saw her smile as she trailed her fingertips across his chest. "I made a decision to go after what I wanted."

"Well, it was a great idea."

She pushed up on one elbow and looked down at him. "I certainly think so." Stretching, she nearly purred, "God, I feel fabulous."

"Look pretty good, too."

"Thanks." She gave his flat belly a gentle pat and sat up. "Wow, Mandy was right."

"I'm sorry?" Confusion rang in his tone. "Your sister was right about what, exactly?"

"That there is no substitution for great sex."

"I can agree to that." He watched her as she slid off the bed, stretched lazily, then walked to the French doors and the balcony beyond. Damn, she made a hell of a picture. Her body was riper than it had once been and every new curve looked fantastic on her.

"I always loved this room," she said as she walked, stark naked, into the late evening.

His heart jumped. "Yeah, well, good thing the

balcony only faces the ocean or you'd be putting on quite a show."

She looked back at him over her shoulder and shook her hair back from her face. Grinning, she pointed out, "That's exactly what I love about this room. Complete privacy."

"Yeah, unless there's someone out there in a boat with a telescope or binoculars."

Frowning a little—not that he was a prude or anything—Jack got off the bed, yanked on his slacks and carried his shirt with him as he went to join her. Her skin was practically glowing, he thought wildly as he approached her. Her face lit up with her smile and her hair was lifting into a blond dance in the wind brushing past her.

"Come on. Put this on," he muttered, holding his shirt for her.

"Spoilsport," she said, but complied, slipping into the black shirt that was so long on her, it hit her midthigh. "This view is breathtaking."

"Yeah," he agreed, leaning against the railing as he looked at her. "Really is."

Her lips twitched. "I was talking about the ocean and how it looks just as the stars are appearing. Just before the moonlight."

"I was talking about you."

She turned to meet his gaze and her eyes softened. "Now you're being nice," she said. "I'm never sure what to make of you when you're being nice."

He choked out a laugh. "Is it so hard to believe?"

"Hard, no. Just…unexpected."

"Well then, I'm sorry about that."

She shoved both hands through her hair and said, "Wow. Nice *and* an apology."

That stung, but he really couldn't blame her for it, he supposed. He'd left her seven years ago. And he hadn't been *nice* about it, either.

"Don't look so stricken, Jack," she said. "I stopped being mad at you a long time ago."

"I didn't leave to hurt you, Serena," he said, his voice so low now it was almost lost in the rush of wind and the soft sigh of the waves against the shore.

"I know that." She shrugged, and even that tiny movement stirred his blood again. "Now, I mean. I didn't then. You broke my heart."

He'd known that, but hearing it said stabbed a spear of ice through him.

"Looking back," Serena mused, "I can actually see why you left."

"Is that right?" Intrigued now, he said, "Tell me."

She smiled, but it was just a little sad, and that tugged at something inside him whether he wanted it to or not. "Oh, God, when I remember, I can see myself, so eager, so completely in love with you that all I could focus on was the future that my busy little brain had built up for us."

He remembered, too. Her heart in her eyes whenever she looked at him. The way she would lay out their future right down to the color of their kids' bedrooms. Yeah, he wasn't ashamed to admit that it had terrified him at the time. Plus, there was the unhappiness of his family hanging over his head and the absolute *misery* of his parents' marriage as a shining example of what not to do with your life.

Yeah. He'd run. And he hadn't been kind when he left, and though it made him a bastard, he couldn't regret leaving. Only the way he'd done it.

"You're still looking at me like I'm a puppy you accidentally kicked."

His frown deepened. "You're no puppy, Serena, and I want you to know I'm not sorry I left—"

"Okay…"

"But I didn't have to be such a dick about it, either."

She laughed. "This really is an amazing night. Great sex. Apologies. And you being nice to me. All that's missing is some wine." She tipped her head. "Have any?"

God, Serena in this mood was irresistible. He wondered if she knew what she was doing to him, then realized she would have to know. She was looking at him, wasn't she? So that led to another question. One he'd already asked himself. What was she up to? What had prompted this change?

"I think I can manage some wine." He turned for the bedroom. "White or red?"

"Choices, choices," she said, smiling. "White."

He nodded, then left her there on the balcony with the twilight falling around her. Jack made it to the kitchen downstairs in record time, grabbed some glasses, a cold bottle from the fridge and a bag of pretzels—best he could do on short notice—from the pantry. Then he headed back up.

When he walked into the bedroom, he simply stopped and stared at the woman out on his balcony. As the rising moon crept higher, she was as still as a statue and yet as vibrant as any woman had ever been. Life simply pulsed around her and he felt inexorably drawn to her.

For seven years, she'd been a memory that had, occasionally, haunted him, and now that he'd had her again, he couldn't imagine losing her as he once had. Hell, he wanted her again already. Usually, once he'd been with a woman he desired, that itch was scratched and he was ready to move on. But with Serena, it was more. Always had been.

Damn it.

"Are you just going to stand there?" she asked without turning to look at him. "Or are you going to pour the wine?"

Shaking his head, he walked toward her. "You have radar or something?"

"Or something."

Then she did turn to smile at him and *something* inside Jack fisted around his heart. And he wasn't happy about it. He still didn't trust "love." But *love* wasn't on the table, was it? No one was talking about forever. This was great sex and an intimate relationship with a woman he found…fascinating.

He walked toward her, saw that smile of hers and told himself that sex didn't mean commitment. Sex wasn't a promise of a future or that fairy-tale ending she'd talked about the other day. Sex just… *was*. And he wanted more of it. With Serena.

"You look so serious," she said as he approached. "Does this mean your *nice* period is over?"

He set the glasses and the bag of pretzels on the table, then went to work on removing the cork. "I'm always nice."

"Ah. Then I guess I just have to pay closer attention."

He laughed shortly, pulled the cork free and poured each of them a glass of cold, straw-colored wine. Handing her one of them, he saw her glance at the table.

"Pretzels?"

"They were handy."

"I like pretzels." She reached for one and took a bite.

Why did that look sexy?

"I'll call for takeout in a while."

"Chinese?"

"Sure." He brushed that aside for the moment just to look at her and try to figure out where they were going from here. "Look, maybe we should talk."

She laughed softly and gave her head a shake, throwing her hair back from her face. "And now for the *after-sex* talk meant to let me down gently?"

God, was he frowning again? Deliberately, he relaxed his features and said, "That's not what I meant to say."

"Okay." A soft chuckle rustled from her throat. "What would you say, Jack?"

At the moment, staring into her beautiful eyes, damned if he could think of a thing.

She took a sip of wine, smiled, then looked at him over the rim of the crystal. "Do you want to remind me that you're just not the marrying kind?"

Jack watched her and tried to figure out what she was thinking. In the old days, he would have known—mainly because she'd have blurted out everything she was feeling at the time. This Serena, though, continually surprised him. He liked it. Well, except for right now.

He sighed a little and briefly turned his face into the breeze sliding in from the ocean before looking back at her. "Serena, this is not what I meant by talking."

"Oh. Okay." She smiled again and tipped her head to watch him. "Maybe you want to tell me that you'll be rushing back to Europe?"

"No." Why was it he was suddenly feeling like a fool when his only plan had been to have a conversation about where this was headed? If anywhere.

"Well, what's left, Jack?"

He took a long gulp of his wine and felt that icy liquid slide through his system. "I just think we should know where we stand. That's all."

"We stand where we have for the last seven years," she said. "Alone." She reached out and briefly laid one hand on his forearm before releasing him and stepping back. "Jack, this doesn't make us a couple. It makes us lovers. At least for tonight."

Another surprise. The Serena he knew was not a one-night-stand kind of woman. He really didn't know what to make of any of this and that left him feeling more than a little off balance. He narrowed his eyes on her as if he could see into her mind if he just worked at it hard enough. "And that's all you're interested in? Tonight?"

"Were you thinking something else?"

Was he? No. Of course not. There was something between them, he knew. But was it more than sex? How the hell could he know that?

"I don't know what I'm saying anymore," he admitted with a scowl. "You're confusing me. Serena, you're not sounding like yourself at all."

"That's because I'm not the same woman you used to know." She took a sip of wine, then turned her face toward the ocean, where waves rolled end-lessly toward the shore in a rhythm that was like the heartbeat of the world. "Jack, this isn't just about me. Or you, for that matter. I'm a mom."

"Yeah, I know. Alli's great."

She smiled. "Yes, she is. And I won't have her hurt."

Shocked, he said, "I'd never hurt her."

Serena looked at him. "Not intentionally, no. But if I let you back in and you left again, she might get her heart broken, and I can't—won't—risk that."

"So tonight's it." His fingers tightened on the stem of the wineglass. Disappointment reared up inside him and Jack ground his teeth together to swallow back whatever else he might have said. What would have been the point? How had everything gone from great to crap in just a few minutes?

"Tonight, yes." She looked up at him. "And any other night we might want to share. But sex is all there is, Jack. I don't want anything else from you."

"Well, that's great," he said, with a little less enthusiasm than he might have thought. He took another long sip of wine. "Then we know where we stand."

Jack couldn't believe that *he* had just gotten the speech he'd given way too many women over the years. Hell, it was basically what he'd said to Serena seven years ago. Was this some weird sort of Karma? Or just cosmological payback? Either way, he didn't much like it. Now he had a glimmer of how she must have felt when he'd walked away from her.

"Exactly." She smiled at him, as if he were a kid getting an A on a test, then held out her glass for more wine.

As he poured, he looked into her eyes and saw just what she wanted him to see, he thought. She had changed. A lot. Where he used to see love and anticipation glittering in her eyes, now there was... carefree warmth with no expectations. Where that left them—him—he had no idea.

"So," she said after a sip of wine, "you want to order dinner first? Or should we wait until after we go again?"

Yeah, confusion reigned inside him until he was faced with that particular question. Then he had absolutely no doubts about what would come next. Jack set his wineglass on the table and reached for her.

"After," he said. "Definitely after."

Eight

The gala was inching closer—just a few days away now, and the Careys were closing ranks. Happened every year, Serena told herself a week later. Yes, the last week with Jack had been… illuminating. She hadn't realized just how much she'd missed him. And Mandy had been right. There was just nothing better than great sex.

They hadn't "talked" again since that first night, and she hadn't had him come to her home because she was still worried about protecting Alli from caring for someone only to see him disappear from her life. But every night, she'd been with him. In that wonderful bedroom with a view of the sea.

On that fabulous bed with a man who could set her on fire with a single look.

Was she a little worried that she was feeling more for him than she'd planned to? Of course. But that worry wasn't enough to keep her away. For as long as it lasted, she and Jack would use each other, and when it ended this time...*she* would be the one walking away.

Meanwhile, the gala had to be her first priority at the moment. She was going to make sure this year's event was the best one they'd ever held. *Her* name was attached to it this time and she was going to make a statement with it.

So the extra family meetings were just one more hurdle to get past.

"I don't understand, Candy," Martin muttered. "Why are you spending so much time on this competition? You're never at home. I'm eating dinner by myself almost every night."

Serena's mother gave her husband a dumbfounded stare. "Says the man who's a ghost in his own home. Martin, you were supposed to retire. Instead, you're busier than ever. Am I supposed to sit at home waiting for you to drop by however briefly? Not going to happen."

"If we could talk about the gala..." Bennett attempted to steer them back on track, but their parents were on an entirely different train.

"That's not fair and you know it," Martin argued, ignoring their children. "I've got things I have to see to before I can leave the business."

"That's bullshit, Marty, and *you* know it."

The whole table went quiet. Candace Carey *never* swore. The entire family stared at her as if seeing her for the first time, but she was oblivious.

"I've been very patient with you, Marty. But that time is done. If I'm supposed to live a life alone, then it's going to be one I choose."

"Alone? Who said you have to live alone?"

"You do. You're never home."

"You know where I am."

"Yes. Not home." Candace gave her husband a steady stare, lifted her chin and said, "Which is why I've decided to move in with Bennett."

"What?" Bennett sounded horrified and who could blame him? "Mom, you can't move in with me."

"Of course I can, dear. You're never there, either." She shook her head in disappointment. "Just like your father."

"Damn it, Candy."

"Don't you swear at me."

"You swore at me first!"

"How did I get dragged into this?" Bennett demanded.

Serena was wondering the same thing.

"Oh, don't burst a blood vessel, Bennett," their mother said, waving his objections away with a flick of an elegantly manicured hand. "Like I said. You're as bad as your father. You're never home. You won't even know I'm there."

"Well, if you'll be alone there," Martin argued, "you can be alone in our home."

"I prefer not," she said primly. Then, glancing at Bennett again, she said, "My bags are packed. I'll be at your home this evening at eight. After the auditions."

For the first time in her life, Serena saw actual *panic* on her older brother's face. If this weren't so weird, it would be funny. Bennett treated his home in Dana Point like the Batcave. As far as she knew, no one in the family had been invited there since he had a tiny housewarming party when he moved in five years ago. For all she knew, he had actual bats hanging from the rafters.

"Mom…" Bennett's voice rang with forced patience.

"I'll make dinner."

Beside Serena, Amanda snorted. That was actually more of a threat than an appeasement. Candace Carey hadn't cooked in thirty years. Their housekeeper took care of the kitchen. Serena wasn't much of a cook, either, but at least she didn't pretend to be. Serena did not envy her older brother.

While her parents argued and Bennett looked like a drowning man going down for the third time, Serena thought this would be a perfect time for their youngest brother to stroll in unannounced. Justin would be enough of a distraction that even their parents would be startled into silence.

But, naturally, Justin didn't show up. He never did, and if he had, Bennett would have erupted on him. So maybe it wouldn't solve the argument problem after all.

"Mom!" Amanda's voice cut through the noise and everyone looked at her. When she had everyone's attention, Amanda continued, "Why don't you tell us about the Summer Stars program? Are you having any trouble dealing with the webmasters?"

"Oh, not at all," Candace said, turning her back on her husband to focus on Amanda. "Chad and I came up with a wonderful new design that he's going to implement tomorrow. We have a lunch meeting today to finalize it."

"Who's Chad?" Martin asked.

"We already have the website up," Bennett pointed out unnecessarily.

"Yes, dear, but it lacked…pizzazz."

Serena grinned at the stupefied look on her brother's face.

"Who's Chad?" Martin asked again.

"If we had just held a virtual fundraiser this year like I wanted to in the first place…" Bennett's muttering was half-hearted and Serena felt sure it was because he was still shocked by his mother's determination to move in with him. She really couldn't blame him.

"That was a ridiculous idea anyway, dear," Candace said, with a slow shake of her head.

"Okay, that's all great, Mom," Amanda said, steering the conversation further away from the tension building in the room. "Serena, anything left to do for the gala?"

"Not a thing," she said, hoping she was right about that. "It's all under control. I'm having my final meeting with Margot tomorrow and I think we're going to really shake things up this year."

"Who's Chad?" Martin was still staring at his wife as if she were a stranger.

Serena ignored the undercurrents and went on. "The photographer is in the pavilion today, deciding how to set up his equipment and where it would be best to hang the screens where we'll be flashing the photos."

"And the raffle?" Bennett asked. "What about Jack's idea? How's that coming?"

Jack.

He hadn't been off her mind in days. Ever since she'd decided to finally just go for it so she could put the man firmly behind her—oh, God, there was a mental image for the ages—she hadn't been able to stop thinking of him. Especially since she was spending hours with him every night only to drive home and crawl into an empty bed alone.

"Earth to Serena."

She blinked and looked up at Bennett. "What?"

"The raffle? The big giveaway? Jack Colton? Ring a bell?"

"Several," she admitted, then silently added, *Though not for any of the reasons you brought up.*

"Great," Bennett said. "How about you share some of them?"

Amanda gave her foot a nudge under the table and she was pretty sure she caught a gleam of interest in her mother's eyes. Oh, she didn't want Candace figuring out what was going on. She didn't need family input in a situation she was already blindly stumbling through.

"Sure, Bennett. To business."

"That is the point of this meeting, right?" he asked.

"Yes. Okay then, the giveaway is going to be huge." She really hated that Jack had been right about his idea.

After she and her assistant had gone over the specs and pictures of the hotels Jack was offering as prizes, Serena knew that this hotel raffle was going to be the hit of the gala. And though it irked her to admit it, she also enjoyed knowing that it was going to help her make this gala the best one in years.

Which was also irritating, because she'd needed Jack to put her over the top.

Serena laid it all out for the family, sliding pictures across the table so everyone could see the properties for themselves. "Jack's offering stays at his hotels in the US and in Europe. I think our patrons are going to love trying to win one of the twelve one-week packages." She looked at Bennett and nodded. "You guys were right. We're going to raise a fortune on the raffle alone."

Nodding, Bennett gave her a brief smile of approval and moved on to their mother. "The auditions still panning out?"

"Oh, yes, we've had some wonderful performers. A few clinkers, too, but God love them. At least they had the courage to go after what they wanted."

"What's that supposed to mean, Candy?" Martin leaned over the table and glared at his wife. "I do go after what I want."

"Yes. As long as it's rooted in the Carey Center."

"Can we not?" Bennett asked, then went on without waiting for an answer. "If that's it for today, I've got an appointment, and if I don't leave now, I'll be late."

"Who's the appointment with?"

"Marty," Candace said, "why do you care? Your son is in charge. You trained him. You taught him. Let him be in charge."

"He is in charge. I'm just asking questions and offering my perspective."

"I don't have time for this," Bennett said, already headed to the door. He stopped when his mother spoke again.

"None of us has time for this." Candace stood up and glared at her husband. "You're hopeless, Martin. You'll never retire. You'll expect me to be at home. Alone. Waiting for you to drop by. Well, I'm tired of being alone, Marty."

All of them stared at Candace, hardly able to believe what they were hearing.

"Which is exactly why I'm moving in with our son."

Bennett's head hit his chest. "Mom…"

"It'll be fine, Bennett. We'll have a wonderful time. Maybe with me there, you'll come home more often than your father does." Then she whirled around and headed out the door. "Come along, Bennett." As they left, the rest of them heard her say, "I'll take the guest room at the front of the house, Bennett. There's a lovely view and…"

"What is wrong with you women?" Martin asked his daughters when the others were gone.

"Nothing is wrong with us, Dad," Serena said. "It's not a battle of the sexes here. It's you versus Mom and I think she's right."

"I'm out of this." Amanda sat back and crossed her arms over her chest.

"It's so wrong for a man to love the company he built up from nothing?" Martin argued, and he threw a frustrated glance at the empty doorway through which his wife had left.

"Maybe it's time to love the wife who helped you do it," Serena said.

"What kind of thing is that to say?" Martin shoved his chair back and jumped to his feet. "Of course I love her. Why would I give a damn about why she's so damn mad all the time if I damn well didn't love her?"

Serena not only heard the frustration in his voice, she could see it all over his face. And she felt bad for him. But at the same time, she wanted to kick him. "Dad, if you don't find a way to let go of the company and grab hold of Mom, you might lose both."

"Damned if I will," he grumbled and left under a full head of steam.

A second or two of silence followed his exit until Amanda turned to her and said, "This is not going to end well."

Jack had had enough of the sneaking-around-only-meet-at-his-place thing he and Serena had going on. He wasn't sure why it bothered him, but it did. She didn't want him at her house. Around her daughter. And that was a thorn digging at him, too.

Hell, Serena was calling the shots in this…

whatever it was between them, and that was going to stop today. She'd been in charge long enough and it was damn well time that *both* of them started making the decisions. So, Jack had decided to change things up. Which was why he stood outside Serena's penthouse door holding a giant bouquet of flowers and a teddy bear.

A few seconds after he knocked, the door swung open and he looked down to see a beautiful little girl staring up at him through wide blue eyes. She grinned, clearly delighted. "Jack!"

"That's right—" He broke off when he heard Serena's voice.

"Alli, you know you're not supposed to answer…" Her voice trailed off when she spotted him. "Jack? What're you doing here?"

Serena wore skintight cream-colored leggings with a soft pale lemon off-the-shoulder T-shirt. Her feet were bare and her toes were painted a dark rose. Her hair was loose, and though she wore no makeup, she was still the most beautiful woman he'd ever seen. For a moment, his mouth dried up and his heartbeat hammered in his ears.

Alli reached up and tugged at her mother's shirt. "He's my friend. He came to see me."

Serena sighed and looked up at him. "Jack…"

He grinned at Alli and ignored her mother. "You're right. I did come to see you."

"And you brought me a present!" She bounced

a little while she eyed the teddy bear and Jack smiled even wider. He'd never been around kids much, but Serena's daughter had so much charm he couldn't resist her.

"Now, maybe I brought you the flowers and your mom the teddy bear," he said.

Alli laughed in delight. "You're silly."

"I guess I am," he agreed and went down on one knee in front of her. "So I suppose the teddy bear must be for you." He held it out to her and Alli swept it into a huge hug and buried her face in its fur.

When she looked up again, she gave him another bright smile, then threw herself at him, wrapping her free arm around his neck and squeezing. "Thank you, Jack!" She let him go and turned to her mother. "I'm gonna show Teddy my room!"

"Okay," Serena said, but the little girl had already dashed off, chattering to the bear in her arms.

"Well, that was sneaky," Serena murmured.

"Hey, I tried to give you the bear," he said when she turned back to him.

She sighed. "Jack, you shouldn't be here."

He leaned against the doorjamb and let his gaze slide up and down her body, taking the time to relish the view before meeting her gaze again. "Yeah, I got tired of hiding out at my house."

She frowned a little, then squared her shoulders. "I told you when this started that—"

"That you don't want Alli hurt."

"Exactly."

"Bringing her a teddy bear won't hurt her," he said softly.

"No, but if she cares for you and you disappear, she will be hurt."

"I get that," he said, his gaze locked with hers. "But I'm not going to hurt her. I'm not going to disappear."

"You did seven years ago," she pointed out.

"Yeah, well, a lot of things have changed since then, haven't they?"

She was still meeting his gaze, so he saw her eyes flare and he knew she was thinking about everything that had been happening between them since they'd reconnected. Well, hell, it was good to know he wasn't the only one.

"Why don't you let me in and we'll talk."

Her lips twitched. "Another *talk*?"

He gave her a half smile. "Maybe it'll go better than the last one."

"Maybe." Then she looked at the flowers he held. "You remembered that yellow roses are my favorite."

"I remember a lot of things." He handed her the roses, then walked inside when she backed up for him.

"It's a great place," he said, looking around the purely feminine condo. From the rose-colored sectional to the jewel-toned rugs on the wood floor to the landscapes hanging on the walls, it spoke of elegance and a woman who knew what she wanted.

"Thanks. I'll just put these in water. My housekeeper has the night off, so if you're planning to stay for dinner, it's my turn to call for delivery."

He laughed and took a seat on the massive L-shaped sofa. Draping one arm along the back, he looked up at her and said, "One of us should learn how to cook."

"Why? We both know how to dial."

"Good point." She disappeared into what he guessed was the kitchen, and while she was gone, he took the time to look around. It was what he would have expected from Serena. Quiet. Classy. When he spotted the French doors leading to a balcony, he began to stand to go check out her view.

"Jack!" Alli ran into the room, the teddy bear hooked under one arm and a book in her other hand. "Read me a story!"

He watched her clamber up onto the couch and buried that tiny spurt of…fear? He liked Alli a lot, but he wasn't exactly used to dealing with kids. Still. How hard could it be?

"Sure." He looked at the book. *The Lost Puppy.* "You like puppies?" Stupid question.

"I'm gonna get a puppy."

"Really?"

She nodded so hard, her pigtails flew on either side of her face. Jack smiled because for such a tiny thing, she looked fierce, and he wondered if Serena had been the same when she was a child.

"I thought you wanted a castle like your friend."

She gave him a calculated smile. "She has a castle *and* a puppy."

"Ah." This little girl would go far.

Carrying Teddy with her, Alli snuggled up to his side, leaned her head on his shoulder and ordered, "Read."

"Right." He opened the book and looked down at the child pressed to his side.

Her breathing was soft and steady, her arm wrapped hard around the teddy bear, and the scent of her shampoo wafted up to him. Her gaze was focused on a book that was clearly her favorite, judging by the worn pages and cracked spine. While he read the story about a puppy trying to find its way home, Alli snuggled closer to him and Jack felt an unexpected hard tug of warmth in his heart.

The little girl, all big eyes and bright smile, had decided she could trust him, and that was a gift he hadn't been given since her mother had done the same and he'd tossed that trust back in her face. Shame briefly flitted through him, but he pushed it aside. There was no changing the past.

He also wasn't sure he deserved Alli's trust, but

he was going to make damn sure he didn't abuse it. He wrapped his right arm around her and held her close as she laid her head on his chest and stared at the book with eyes full of wonder. That tug on his heart came harder. Stronger.

He liked it.

And where the hell did that leave him?

He glanced up when he felt Serena's presence, and there she was, in the open doorway to the kitchen. Holding a crystal vase with yellow roses spearing up from it, she was watching him with Alli and her eyes were soft and…worried.

Hell. So was he.

"Mommy! Jack's reading about my puppy!"

"Alli…" Serena smiled at her daughter. "We talked about this. We can't get a puppy right now. We don't have a yard for him to play in."

Jack watched the back-and-forth between mother and daughter, and if there was a bet, he would have put his money on Alli. Who could look into that face and say *no*?

"He can play on the roof with me," the girl said slyly.

"Alli…"

"Jack likes puppies." She turned her face up to him and he was toast. If it were up to him, he'd be running out to the closest shelter to bring her a puppy of her own. But, he reminded himself, it was not up to him.

"It's up to your mom, Alli."

She pouted, her shoulders drooped and she sighed heavily. Oh, yeah, she was very good.

"When Jack finishes the book," Serena said, "it's time for dinner and a bath."

"Can we have tacos?"

Serena sighed, glanced at Jack and asked, "Tacos all right with you?"

"Tacos!" Alli shouted.

"Even if they weren't," Jack said with a grin, "I'd never admit it now."

"You are easy," Serena said, carrying the vase of flowers into the room to set on a table against the wall.

"I've got a soft spot for pretty blondes," he confessed.

She turned slowly around to face him and her gaze locked with his. "For how long?" she wondered.

And that, he thought, was a very good question.

Nine

Two days before the gala, everything went to hell.

"It was perfect," Serena complained, stalking around Amanda's office. She just resisted tugging at her hair. To be this close to pulling off the gala in grand fashion only to watch it explode was infuriating and frustrating and— "It was set. Everything was done. It was going to be great and now we don't have a *band*?"

Amanda perched on the edge of her desk and watched Serena's frantic pacing. "So why did the band back out?"

Serena waved one hand in the air. "Something about being offered a European tour."

"Wow, and they didn't turn that down to play at our fundraiser? Selfish bastards."

Serena stopped, shot her sister a glare and then kept walking. "Fine. Great for them. Sucks for me."

"There must be other bands available."

"Oh, sure. With two days' notice, there's lots of fantastic bands just sitting around, waiting for someone to call." She stopped pacing, put her hands on her hips and took several deep breaths. "I can't believe this is happening." She looked at her sister. "What am I going to do?"

"Well, stop panicking," Amanda said. "That's not helping."

"Do you think I don't know that? You know what else isn't helping? Mom offered to call the band we've used for years." She threw both hands in the air. "*Of course*, the Swing Masters are available! Nobody wants to hire them!"

"Well, that was mean," Amanda said softly. "Accurate, but mean."

"I can't tell Bennett," Serena continued as if her sister hadn't spoken. "I'll never hear the end of it. *And* he might side with Mom about hiring the old band. You just never know what the hell Bennett's going to do."

"True. Plus, now that Mom's moved in with him, he's on edge all the time." Amanda shivered. "Henry called him last night and Bennett started raving about Mom hiring painters to come in and redo his place because, and I quote, *it's too grim*."

"Not grim, really. Just…beige," Serena said. "A lot of beige, as I remember it."

"Yeah. It's more boring than grim." Nodding, Amanda said, "The upside here is she moved in with Bennett and not one of us."

"Points for me not having a guest room."

"And me living with Henry." Amanda got a little starry-eyed, gave a quiet little sigh while her mouth curved in what could only be yearning. Serena snapped her fingers in her sister's face.

"Hey! Back from your daydreams about Henry. I've got problems here."

"Right. Well, hey, maybe Henry knows some-one—"

Serena thought about that for a minute and shook her head. Henry wasn't the answer. She'd seen him dance and it looked as though he'd never heard of music. Jack might be the answer, though. Oh, she really didn't want to have to ask him for help. But she only had two days to pull off something amazing. If she didn't have help with this, she'd have to tell Bennett, and there was no way she was going to do that.

"I'll have to ask Jack," she muttered.

"That's a great idea."

"No, it's not." Sighing, Serena considered her

options. She'd been getting in deeper and deeper with Jack over the last week or more.

And since the night he'd shown up at her house uninvited, he'd managed to come back twice. Alli was crazy about him. Even Sandy, her housekeeper, was charmed by Jack. It was only Serena holding out now and she had to. Because she'd finally had to admit the truth to herself, if no one else.

The night she came into the room to find Jack reading to Alli and her baby girl curled up trustingly to his side, that one undeniable truth had dropped onto Serena's head like a brick wall.

She was still in love with Jack.

Watching Alli snuggled up to Jack while he read to her about the puppy she was determined to have had touched Serena more than she would have thought possible. Her little girl had never known a daddy, and she had apparently chosen Jack to be the one she wanted. And Serena was torn. She wanted to believe in Jack. To love him completely as she once had. But Alli's heart was even more tender than her own, and how could she take the risk?

Loving Jack was, apparently, inevitable for Serena. But trusting him was something else.

"Hello, Serena. Are you in there?" Amanda quipped.

Serena blinked out of her scattered thoughts and stared at her sister.

Pushing one hand through her hair, Serena said, "Sorry. Mind is just racing and—"

"It's Jack."

"Yes, Jack," she agreed. "I have to ask him for help with the stupid band."

"Not what I meant," Amanda said, smiling. "You're in love with him."

"What?" Serena shook her head and hoped she was believable in her denial. "Don't be ridiculous."

Amanda eased off the edge of the desk and walked toward her. "I'm not. I'm being extremely perceptive. I can't believe I didn't notice before this."

Oh, God. She really didn't need Amanda teasing her about this. "Stop it, okay? Just because you're nuts about Henry doesn't mean everyone else is in love."

"Not everyone," Amanda mused, "just you."

She could keep denying it, but what would be the point? Besides, now that Amanda had noticed, she wouldn't let it go. Really, Serena was lucky no one else had noticed. Especially Jack.

"Fine. I love him. But that doesn't change anything."

Amanda stared at her, baffled. "How are we related? Love changes *everything*."

"No." On this, Serena was very firm. "Okay, yes, I love Jack," and just saying it out loud made it all so real it was nearly terrifying. "But I can't risk Alli's feelings."

"Come on. Jack would never hurt her."

"Not on purpose. Of course not. But when he leaves again, then what? Alli's heart's broken."

"Sure it's Alli's heart you're worried about?"

Serena narrowed her eyes on her sister. "What's that supposed to mean?"

"It means you're sounding like the old Serena, not the new-and-improved version."

"You're not helping."

"I'm trying to," Amanda said.

"I meant with the band situation."

"Screw the band."

"Easy for you to say."

Amanda sighed. "You came a long way over the last seven years, Serena. You went out and took charge of an affair that turned into love and now you've scared yourself. You don't want to go backward with the band? Well, don't go backward with yourself, either."

Serena hated that her sister had a point, but she didn't really have the time right now to think about what Amanda was saying. Once the gala was over and things had settled down, then she'd be able to give plenty of thought to the situation with Jack.

"Look, I get it. And I promise I'll consider every-thing you said. *After* the gala."

"Fine. Go. Call Jack."

Her head dropped back. "God, I really don't want to." Sighing, she added, "I'm going to make some more calls. See what I can find on my own."

"You've got two days, Serena."

"Thanks. I know." *Two days.* Not a lot of time and it was ticking past really quickly.

When she left her sister, she went straight to her office only to find Jack waiting for her. Was the universe screwing with her? Or was it sending her a sign? Either way, it was a little unsettling. "Why are you here?"

"Good to see you, too," he said, tucking his phone into his suit pocket. He stood up as she closed the office door behind her. "We had a lunch date, remember?"

"God, I completely forgot." She rubbed the spot between her eyes.

"Headache?" Jack asked.

"You have no idea." She leaned one hip against her desk. In a few minutes, she told him everything. As much as she didn't want to have to ask for help, she knew she needed it. And she actually felt better, spelling it all out for him.

"So, basically, you just need a band for the gala."

"Just?" she repeated, dumbfounded. Had he not been listening? Was the panic in her voice undetectable to him? "*Just?* Yes, I need a band. It's two days away, I can't find a decent band that isn't already booked, and if I don't, the whole thing is going to be a disaster."

He grinned.

She scowled at him. "This isn't funny, Jack."

"No, but not a tragedy, either." He grabbed his phone again and started scrolling through his contacts. "Because *you* have *me*. I know some people who might be able to help."

He stepped away, hit the speed dial and waited for his old friend to answer. When he did, Jack smiled.

"Tom. It's Jack. Listen," he said briskly, "I've got a situation and I need your help." In a few short sentences, he explained the problem to the man, then listened while the other man talked.

Jack watched Serena pace as he answered Tom's questions. She was worried, a little panicked and, clearly, not exactly thrilled to accept help from him.

They'd been together again for more than a week. But there was more than the past week between them. There was chemistry. Magic. And something more that even he could feel. Yet she was holding back. Keeping him in a separate corner of her life where he couldn't interfere in the rest of her world. Hell, he'd be surprised if her family knew they were together again.

And as that thought spilled through his mind, he had to wonder if they *were* together. Sure, they had great sex almost every night, but that was as far as it went. There was no staying overnight. No sharing of everyday stuff. They never made plans together beyond the next night. There was no talk of a future. No pretense of being in a relationship. No trust.

That last word resonated in his mind because he knew that it was his own damn fault that she didn't trust him. She had once, he remembered. Until he'd walked out on her and all of her plans for their future.

She stopped pacing suddenly and turned to look at him, and his heart simply turned over in his chest. It seemed that every time he saw her, there was *more for him to feel*. Serena Carey was still the most beautiful woman he'd ever seen. And in the last seven years, she'd become even more lovely. Everything about her appealed to him. Everything in him responded to her in ways that he never had with anyone else.

He hadn't wanted this and wasn't sure what to do about it now that these *feelings* were swarming through him.

Jack didn't trust feelings. Hell, they'd never done his parents any good. He'd seen love used as a weapon. He'd seen it left to die and wither. His own parents' marriage had been a misery and the one thing he didn't want to do was continue that tradition. So where did that leave him?

"What?" His friend's voice in his ear brought him out of his thoughts and Jack focused on what he was saying. "Seriously? Yeah. It's a benefit for kids and they do really great work. The band canceling at the last minute is going to seriously hurt things for those kids. They really depend on the money raised at the Carey event. Who? Yeah. Okay."

Serena's gaze was trained on him, hope shining in her eyes.

"That's great." He grinned. Tom's brother managed some of the best bands in the world. If anyone could help them out, it would be him. Looked like this was going to work out. "Yeah. I owe you." He laughed and shook his head. "Anytime. Sure. One-week stay at the Tuscany hotel for you and your wife. Least I can do. You got it. Thanks."

He hung up and Serena was on him in a flash. "One-week stay in Tuscany?"

"Seems only fair." Jack shrugged. "He got you a band. They're on a break from their US tour and they're happy to do benefits."

"Oh, God." She stared at him as if he'd lost his mind. "You agreed without even telling me who the band is? How could you do that? Who is it? When will they be here?"

He laughed a little and tucked his phone away. "Yes, I agreed. They'll be here tomorrow to set up for the gala performance. And you're going to approve. I guarantee it."

She closed her eyes and took a deep breath. *"Who?"*

"Black Roses."

Her eyes flew open and her jaw dropped. "Are you serious? They're the most popular band on the planet. How did you do that?"

"Tom's brother is their manager and—" The rest of his answer was lost when she threw herself at him, wrapped her arms around his neck and kissed him, long and hard.

Every brain cell simply went into a coma and he would have dared any man to react differently— if he'd been able to manage a single thought. Instead, he just wrapped his arms around her waist and held her to him, relishing the moment.

When she finally pulled her head back to grin up at him, Serena said, "I can't believe this, Jack. Black Roses? People will be talking about this event for *years*."

"So you're happy?"

"Beyond."

"Happy looks good on you," he murmured, his gaze moving over her face.

"I didn't want to ask you—or anyone—for help," she admitted, still staring into his eyes. "I wanted to handle this mess myself."

"You are."

"No." She shook her head. "I needed help. And you were there. I won't forget that."

"Asking for help isn't failing, Serena."

"I know that. But it's not handling it all your-self, either."

"Nobody does," he countered. "You have an as-sistant, don't you?"

"Sure, but not the same thing."

"Exactly the same thing." He kissed her fore-head. "None of us gets this stuff done without help. Hell, if you could do it all yourself, you wouldn't need an office building filled with employees."

"You're oversimplifying."

"And you're overcomplicating."

"Because I disagree with you?"

"No." He looked down at her. "What's going on with you? A minute ago, you were thrilled. Now… It's not just accepting help, is it?" he asked as the truth began to dawn on him. "It's accepting help from *me*."

"You know what?" Serena stepped back and away from him. "I don't want to argue. I'm grate-ful for the band, but I've got a ton of minutiae to take care of before the gala, so thank you, but you'd better go."

Jack studied her for a long minute. For a mo-ment there, they'd almost been a team. Then it was gone, and, damn it, he wanted it back. But clearly now wasn't the time for that conversation. "All right. But how about dinner tonight? We can take

Alli to the Burger Barn. She loves those strawberry shakes."

"I don't think so, Jack. But thanks." Walking
back to her desk, she seemed to pull inside herself,
and he didn't like it. "Like I said, I've got a ton of
things to do, so…"

"Fine. Then the night of the gala, I'll pick you
up—"

"No, I'll have to be here early, making sure
things are as they should be."

"It's not a one-woman show, Serena," he said and
hated the tightness in his own voice. He also hated
that there was almost a chill in the room from the
ice that had suddenly seemed to envelop her. She
really didn't like the fact that he'd been the one to
help her out. Was it so hard for her to accept anything from him? "You don't have to do it alone."

"Oh, I won't. The family always arrives early
to check things out." Seated behind her desk, she
looked up at him. "Thank you for the band."

"You're welcome." How did things get so stiff
and impersonal between them in a matter of seconds? Hell, his lips were still burning from that
kiss she'd planted on him, and now she was dismissing him as if it had never happened. "I'll just
see you at the gala, then."

She nodded. "Oh, I'm sure we'll run into each
other."

He'd make damn sure of it.

* * *

The Carey Center was even more beautiful than usual.

As she walked the rooms and the garden area, Serena gave herself a mental pat on the back for pulling this off. She'd taken a chance by shaking things up. New florist. New caterer. The photographer. All of it designed to bring new life to their most important charitable event of the year.

She even had the top band in the world playing for them tonight.

Thanks to Jack. She frowned a little, as she had to admit that without his help this night might have turned out much differently. She could be standing in the middle of a disaster right now instead of feeling triumphant.

As it was, the scents wafting from the food stations were insanely tempting. The flower arrangements were breathtaking, and on stage, Black Roses' road crew were handling the setup of the equipment and running a last-minute sound check.

Servers were all dressed in black slacks, white shirts and red vests and were being given their assignments by the catering service, and the dance floor gleamed like warm honey under the lights.

"Congratulations, sweetie." Amanda came up beside her and gave her a quick one-armed hug. "It looks amazing. I'm seriously going to hire this florist for our wedding."

"Thank God," her fiancé, Henry, said from behind her. "One decision finally made."

Amanda turned and grinned up at him. "Hey, I'm only getting married once. I want it to be perfect."

"If you're there," Henry assured her, "it will be."

"You are so sweet…" She sighed and rested her head on his chest.

Serena felt the tiniest twinge of envy for her sister's happy relationship, then tried to put it aside. Tonight wasn't the time for wishes and hopes.

But she hadn't seen Jack in two days. Alli was asking for him and Serena thought this would be a preview of the rest of her life if something happened and Jack left again. Maybe it would just be best to end it all now. Yes, she loved him. Yes, she would long for him forever. But some risks were too hard to take.

"Serena!" Amanda snapped her fingers in front of her face. "Wake up."

"What? Oh, sorry."

"I didn't tell you how gorgeous you look," her sister said. "I *love* that dress."

So did Serena. A deep scarlet, the dress was a floor-length dream. Narrow shoulder straps supported a bodice that was deeply cut yet managed to look…almost modest. A cinched waist and a flowing bell skirt completed it, and the red heels she wore were already killing her feet.

"I love that color of blue on you."

Amanda did a slow turn and Serena noticed that Henry's eyes burned just watching her. In her floor-length royal blue sheath, Amanda looked like a Greek goddess. And Serena couldn't help but feel another quick prick of envy for the love that her sister and Henry shared. They'd been through a lot and had found their way back to each other. She wondered why that couldn't always happen.

"Uh-oh," Amanda whispered, "the troops are here."

Serena followed her gaze to see Bennett, Candace and Martin approaching. The men were especially handsome in their tailored tuxedos and Candace shone like a candle flame in the deep russet gown that clung to her still-impressive figure.

"Sweetie," Candace said, reaching out to kiss her daughter's cheek. "You did it. Everything is lovely and I'm so sorry I gave you such fits over using the new people. The flowers are divine and I can't wait to taste the shrimp I just passed."

"Thanks, Mom." It really had turned out fabulous, she assured herself silently. Once their guests arrived and the music started, the Carey Center would be pulsing with life and hopefully a sense of fun the gala had lacked the last few years.

"You look gorgeous, Mom," Amanda said.

"I tried to tell her that," Martin tossed in. "But she wouldn't believe me. Wouldn't even let me pick her up at Bennett's house so we could come together."

"We're not together, Martin," Candace pointed out. "Remember?"

Bennett took a deep breath, scrubbed the back of his neck as if attacking the tension knots lurking there and threw a desperate look at Amanda. Leaning in, he said, "You've got to take Mom. I don't know how much more I can handle. She's *cooking*, Mandy."

"Nope. You're on your own. Maybe Serena…"

"No room," she said quickly and was so happy she'd only the three-bedroom apartment. They were all spoken for, so she could dodge her brother's pleas guilt-free.

"Look!" Excitement in their mother's voice had them all looking. "It's Justin!"

Serena watched her youngest brother approach, and she had to admit that, for the rebel of the family, Justin wore a tuxedo as if he were born to. Which, she supposed, he had been. His hair was too long, of course, and his easy, casual stride made him look at ease even though she knew he hated gatherings like this one.

He went right up to Candace, kissed her cheek. "Hi, Mom." His gaze swept over the rest of the family quickly and she noted he didn't spend any time on a greeting to Bennett or their father. Grinning at Serena, he said, "The place looks amazing, sis. Nice job."

"Thanks. I didn't think you'd come."

"Can't miss the biggest event of the year," he said.

"But missing family meetings, that's okay," Bennett put in.

"Where have you been?" Martin demanded. "You're a damn Carey, boy. That comes with responsibility."

"Don't do this now, you guys," Amanda said, throwing a quick look around them to make sure none of the servers or anyone else was paying attention.

"They can't help it," Justin said and gave his older brother a grim smile. "Which is why I avoid the meetings."

"Damn it, Justin—"

"Hush, Bennett," their mother said, and he pressed his lips together so tightly it was as if he were physically holding back the words that wanted to fly out of his mouth.

"Justin, honey," Candace said, laying one hand on his arm, "this is such a nice surprise. Where've you been?"

"Mostly La Jolla, Mom," he said.

"Bodysurfing?" Bennett muttered, and Serena gave him an elbow poke.

"Sometimes," Justin admitted happily. "Mostly, I'm working on something."

"What?" Martin demanded. "The Careys don't have any holdings in San Diego County. What are you *working* on?"

Justin nodded at their father, but kept his expression unreadable. "That's a surprise."

"I'm not a child waiting for Christmas," Martin countered. "What the hell is going on?"

"That's what I came to tell you, Dad," he said, then swept his gaze across all of them. "Tell all of you."

"Let's hear it," Bennett muttered, jamming his hands into his slacks pockets.

"I'm going to have an announcement in a few weeks, so you'll have to wait for the full reveal."

"Perfect," Bennett grumbled.

"That's what you came to tell us," Amanda said. "That you can't tell us something?"

Serena felt bad for her little brother. Justin had always been the one to defiantly carve out his own path. Though she'd admired it from time to time, she also had to admit that he sometimes made things tougher on himself than they had to be.

Why not just tell everyone what was going on with him? Why come to the gala only to announce that he wasn't saying a word about what he was up to for another few weeks? What was the point, other than to stir up Bennett and make their father angry and their mother worry?

"Justin," she said, "you're the youngest, but even you're too old to play games."

He winked at her. "Ever the peacemaker. No worries, Serena. I'm not playing." He looked almost… formidable. "I've got some plans that I'm working on, and once they're ready, I'll tell everyone. But I don't need," he added, shooting a look at his brother and father, "unwanted opinions coming down on me while I get things lined up."

"Fine," Bennett told him. "You don't want to be part of the Carey Corporation, that's your business. But stop pretending to be. Claiming you'll be at a meeting and then never showing up—"

"Never said I would be." Justin cut him off. "That's you, Bennett. *Expecting* me to be there and then getting pissed off when I'm not."

He had a point, Serena told herself.

"So we're clear on this," Justin said tightly, "until I make this announcement, I'm not going to be around much, so don't expect me to be."

"If you had the slightest respect for—"

Candace cut Bennett off with a look. "The first of the guests are arriving. I won't have this family putting on a show for our patrons. So, listen up, everyone," she said, fixing her stern stare on each of them in turn. "Smile. Be happy. And have a good time with everyone even if it kills you. Understood?"

No one argued with Candace when she used that tone of voice, so they all mutely nodded.

"Good," Candace said with a sharp nod. "And as for you, Justin. If you don't attend meetings, I don't really care. But you will keep in touch with your family. Clear?"

"Yes, ma'am."

"Fine. Now that that's settled, get out there and mingle with our guests, and for the love of God, look *happy* about it."

It had been a while since Candace had given her family that steely look and direct orders, but some things would always work, apparently. Serena watched her family move off to be Careys. She plastered a smile on her own face and put aside thoughts of her mother living with Bennett, Justin having secrets. And mostly, there was Jack. The man she loved but couldn't trust. The man she wanted but shouldn't have.

The one man.

The only man.

Damn it.

Jack spotted her the moment he stepped into the massive ballroom. The murmuring roar of the crowd, the snatches of laughter and the clink of crystal all served as an undercurrent to the music pouring from the stage. Black Roses had toned down their usual stage presence, considering the venue—after all, it wasn't an actual concert, but a chance for wealthy people to get together and donate tons of money to a charitable cause.

By the looks of the crowd, they very much approved.

High on the walls, massive screens flashed with images taken by the wandering photographer and demonstrated just what a success the evening was by the smiles on those featured. On the dance floor, men in black danced with women wearing a rainbow of colors in a dazzle of movement until the whole scene looked like a Jackson Pollock painting.

But once Jack's gaze landed on Serena, she was the only woman he saw. Her hair was golden and that dark red dress against her pale skin seemed to glow, setting her apart from everyone, as if she moved through the crowd with a spotlight attached to her. He watched her pause, smile, chat with people she knew, then move on, checking to be sure everyone was happy and having fun.

He moved through the crowd with a single-minded determination. Two days he'd been without her and he couldn't remember ever being quite so…lonely. He didn't much care for it.

Seven years before, it had been his idea to end things between them. This time, Serena had shut him out, and he liked that even less. He missed her. Missed Alli. He wandered through that big house on the cliffs, listening to the echoes of his own footsteps. His life had become completely entwined with Serena's and he didn't want that to end. So he had a proposal to make and there was no time like the present to do it.

He caught up to her as she was greeting an older couple, the woman draped in diamonds, the man covering a considerable paunch with a well-tailored tuxedo.

"Oh, Jack!" She looked surprised. Had she really believed he wouldn't come?

"You look amazing," he whispered, and he knew from the flash in her eyes that she'd heard him over the noise in the room.

"Thank you. So do you."

He caught her hand in his, then tugged her toward the dance floor. "Dance with me."

"Oh, I should—"

"Dance. The party's going well. There's nothing for you to worry about, so dance."

She took a breath, considered her options briefly, then nodded. "Okay, just one."

He swung her around, then pulled her close, and they swayed with the music. They were a part of the crowd and yet separate from it. Despite the noise and the mass of people, Jack felt at that moment as if they were alone in the universe. Only her blue eyes looking up at him. The feel of her body pressed to his. Her scent, something earthy and intoxicating drifting through him with every breath he took. She felt right in his arms. It was as if everything in the world had suddenly found its balance after being just a little off-kilter for seven long years.

And he knew he didn't want to lose her. Not again.

"What's going on, Jack?" She tipped her head to one side and that glorious hair of hers slid across her shoulders. "You look so serious all of a sudden."

He swept them into a turn, but kept his gaze fixed on hers. "I am serious." He wanted to find the right words. Wanted to find the right time to say what he'd been thinking. But, lost in the moment, Jack couldn't come up with a subtle way to broach his idea. So he blurted it out. "Serena, I want you and Alli to move in with me."

She stumbled slightly, but his grip on her waist only tightened and he held her more closely.

"You what?"

"I mean it. Serena, I've never meant anything more. I'll build Alli that castle she wants—" At her look of astonishment, he amended, "Fine. I'll hire someone to build that castle she wants. We'll get her a puppy. We'll be together. The three of us."

"Jack…"

"Think about it," he said, then corrected himself.

"No, don't *think. Feel.* We're good together, Serena. You, me, Alli. Move in with me. Give us a chance." The more he thought about it, the better he felt about the idea. They'd be together and she would see that she could trust him again. Eventually.

The music swelled, and Jack steered them around the dance floor while he looked into her eyes, trying to read what she was thinking. But for the first time, her eyes gave nothing away and he found himself holding his breath as he waited what felt like forever for her answer.

"No."

"What?" Stunned, he could only stare at her. "Why the hell not?"

"You almost had me, Jack," Serena said softly, with a shake of her head. "For a second there, I thought— Never mind. But then I realized that all you're offering me is an invitation to play house."

"It's more than that," he argued and wondered how he'd managed to bungle this so completely that she couldn't see how important she was to him. He'd never in his life considered living with a woman. Building something together. Hell, he wanted to be a father to her daughter. He wanted it all. Why couldn't she see that?

She touched his cheek briefly and it felt like a condemnation of sorts. "No, it's not, Jack. There's no commitment. No promise of forever. No proposal. Just move in with you. Bring Alli and we'll pretend we're a unit. A family."

"We wouldn't be pretending," he countered. How could they be having this discussion in the middle of a dance floor while hundreds of people crowded into a massive ballroom all around them? How could she say no to being with him? "You want a proposal?"

"I want a promise," she said.

"Damn it, Serena." He lowered his head, but kept his gaze fixed with hers. "We've both seen terrible marriages up close and personal. How is that an answer to anything? A piece of paper doesn't guarantee happiness, for God's sake, and you should know that. There are no guarantees, if that's what you're looking for."

"I'm not looking for a guarantee, Jack." She took a breath and added, "But how can you keep a promise you never made?" She shook her head again. "You're right, Jack. I had a terrible marriage and you watched your parents implode. But that doesn't mean that the institution itself doesn't work. A marriage is what two people make it, Jack. And they both have to want it to work.

"You don't even want to try, and frankly, I'm not sure I do, either."

"Now you're making no sense." He held her even tighter and still had the sensation that she was slipping away from him. Everything had gone so wrong so quickly. He was watching her, hearing her, and still he couldn't believe what was happening. "You want a proposal but you don't?"

She gave him a slow, sad smile. "I would have preferred you offered me a promise—a chance at forever. But I'm not sure I would have said yes. How can I be?" She stopped moving and the other dancers simply moved around them. "What you're offering me might have won me over seven years ago, but I'm not that woman anymore, Jack. I'm worth more. I expect more. And I won't settle. Not ever again. Not for myself and certainly not for Alli."

"I didn't mean—"

She went up on her toes and kissed his lips briefly. "But now that we have all of this out in the open, I'm happy to keep having an affair with you. Think about it."

When she turned and walked away, Jack simply stood on the dance floor, alone in a sea of swirling, swaying color and sound, and looked like a statue dropped incongruously into the middle of a party.

Well, that worked out fine because he suddenly *felt* as if he were made of stone, too.

The gala went on late into the night, and as he'd suspected they would be, Jack's twelve one-week package giveaways were the hit of the evening. Hundreds of people bought countless raffle tickets in the hopes of winning one of those packages, allowing the Careys to collect half again as many donations as they did every year. The giveaway was the talk of the event, and as he watched Serena present the last of those twelve packages, he felt as if not just the gala was coming to an end.

That scene with Serena played again in his mind and he heard her voice echoing inside him. No. She didn't want to play house. No commitment. No promise.

But the sex could continue.

He should be pleased with that. Why wasn't he? Why did he feel as if he'd missed something? As if she were slipping out of reach while he stood by helplessly?

He didn't like being helpless. Didn't like it at all.

Ten

A week later, Bennett stormed into Amanda's office while she and Serena were congratulating themselves over the successful gala.

"That's it," he proclaimed in a half shout. "I can't take it anymore."

"What are you talking about?" Serena asked.

He looked at her as if she'd lost her mind. "Mom. Of course it's Mom. What else would it be?"

Amanda snorted and he shot her a glare and stabbed his index finger at her. "You can laugh, but she's driving me nuts. She had a *decorator* come to *my* house because she says it's *boring*."

"It is," Amanda said sagely with a nod of her

head. "I mean, I haven't seen it since that one glorious party when you first moved in, but I'm guessing you haven't changed a thing. So, how many shades of beige are there, Bennett?"

"That's not the point." He jammed his hands into his pockets and stalked around the room. "My cook's threatening to quit because Mom won't stay out of the kitchen. Suddenly, she thinks she's Betty Crocker!" He stopped and stared at his sisters. "Last night, she made a casserole that was so bad she had to throw the pan away."

Serena bit down hard on her bottom lip to hide her smile. Honestly, it was fun seeing Bennett so shaken. He was always so in control, so locked down emotionally, that this side of him was downright entertaining. Sure, she felt a little sorry for him, but still…

"I can't take it," he repeated and looked at Amanda. "So it's your turn."

"Oh, no, it's not," she said flatly. "I'm living with Henry now."

"Yeah, in a big damn house by the beach. You've got the room, and better, you've got the patience to deal with Mom while she's having this little revolution of hers."

"Little revolution?" Serena stared at him, angry on her mother's behalf. "Dad's the one who caused this situation. Mom's just reacting to it."

"I knew you'd be on her side." Laying a pleading look on Amanda, he said, "You're running the Summer Sensation. Mom's running the Summer Stars program. It would give the two of you plenty of time to work out any kinks."

"There are no kinks," Amanda countered. "But nice try."

"Come on! Help me here." His jaw tightened, his eyes flashed and he blurted out, "Who's the one who went and got your bike back from the kid who stole it?"

"I was eleven," Amanda pointed out with a sardonic twist to her lips. "I think my debt's been paid."

He dropped into a chair, braced his elbows on his knees and cupped his face in his hands. "I don't know how much longer I can last."

"Then talk to Dad," Serena offered. "Tell him to actually resign and that will get Mom back."

Incredulous, he lifted his head and looked at her. "You really think I *haven't*? He's as stubborn as she is and I'm starting to feel like a worn chew toy being pulled on by two pit bulls."

"God, Bennett, I used to think it would be fun to see you shaken out of your rut, but it's just sad." Amanda looked at him and said, "Go away."

"Thanks very much."

She laughed. "Oh, don't get all offended. I didn't mean now. I meant go. Leave town for a few days.

Go to your cabin up in Big Bear. Just get out of the line of fire for a while."

He thought about that for a long minute or two, then slowly nodded. "Not a bad idea. At least I'll have some damn quiet and I can order in food from the local restaurants."

"There you go. And without you there, Mom won't be trying to cook," Serena said, "so *your* cook will stop threatening to quit."

"That's good. Okay. I'll give her a week off. With pay," he added. "I can make this work." Standing up, he buttoned his suit jacket, inclined his head toward his sisters and said, "I'll be out of here by tomorrow morning. One week. Don't let the company crumble while I'm gone."

"Wow," Amanda whispered when he left the room. "Never thought I'd see Bennett like that."

"Yeah. Taking a week off work? That hasn't happened in years." Serena looked at her sister and said, "He won't know what to do with himself."

"He'll work anyway, I imagine," Amanda mused. "Just like you would."

"Excuse me?"

"Come on." Amanda gave her a slow smile. "Look at you. You're becoming just like him."

Serena was stunned. This she hadn't expected. She wasn't a workhorse like Bennett. She did her job, but she wasn't obsessive about it. Was she?

"I am not," she argued, thinking that she had

a very well-rounded life. "I have a daughter and a life and—"

"And?"

"And there's not a single beige wall in my condo."

Amanda snorted. "Fine, no beige. Everything else, though? The whole work-work-work thing? Hello, Bennett Junior."

"That's not funny."

"Truth rarely is," Amanda said with a smile as she shook her head.

Serena really hated to admit that her younger sister might—key word there, *might*—have a point. But since joining the family company, she had poured herself into the job. Into building a life for herself and for Alli. And maybe she had been a little overeager, but that didn't make her a workaholic, did it?

Serena's mind raced for something else to say and finally came up with only, "So now you're the one with all the answers? Until you and Henry got together again, what were you filling your time with?"

"You have a point, too," Amanda acknowledged, "but the main thrust of that point is that I now *have* a life. You're falling deeper and deeper into Carey corporate structure. Is that really what you want?"

"Of course it is or I wouldn't be doing it."

Right? She made her own decisions now and one of them had been to dive into the business. To stake her own claim on the Carey Corporation and she thought she'd done very well in that respect. Serena had devoted a lot of her time to it. She'd had to. She'd worked her ass off on the gala to prove to her family that she could do the job, and now that she had... What?

Serena frowned to herself, and her mind raced with too many thoughts she didn't much like. True, she didn't spend as much time with Alli as she used to, but that was normal. Other moms worked and took care of their kids.

What was the saying? Quality time over quantity? Didn't that make sense anymore? Then she had to admit she'd always hated that saying.

"What I'm trying to tell you is that I have recently discovered that there is more to life than the Carey Corporation. And," she added, "if you're not careful, you're going to fall down the Bennett rabbit hole and end up with no life at all outside this company."

Serena thought about that and was forced to admit her sister might be on to something. At the moment, she was supposed to be in her office working on the marketing strategy for next fall's concert schedule. She was hardly giving herself enough time to enjoy what she'd pulled off at the gala before jumping back into her next project.

Heck, she'd missed putting Alli to bed the night before because she'd stayed late to work over some numbers with Accounting, and… "Oh, my God. You're right."

"I didn't want to be, believe me. Think about it, though," her sister continued. "Before today, when was the last time Bennett went to the cabin?"

She did try. "I have no idea."

"That's because it's never happened. He bought that cabin claiming that he'd spend time there on the weekends. To maintain a life outside the business." Amanda snorted. "He bought that place nine years ago, keeps a property manager to take care of it, and this is the first time he's been in it himself."

Well, that was all kinds of sad. "Okay. I'll think about what you said."

Actually, she didn't believe she'd be able to *stop* thinking about it now that Amanda had dropped those concerns into her head.

"Good. So on to other news." Amanda leaned forward in her desk chair and propped her elbows on the polished oak surface. "How're things with Jack?"

Serena frowned to herself, remembering Jack's non-proposal at the gala and the way they'd left things between them. It had been a week and he hadn't contacted her. So, apparently, if she didn't go along with his plans, he just pulled away completely. Well, fine. Wasn't that what she was trying to protect her and Alli from in the first place?

Serena missed him. But clearly he wasn't missing her, so how could his idea of the three of them living together mean anything? No, she'd done the right thing, she assured herself silently. She had to protect Alli. Had to protect her own heart from another crushing blow.

It didn't matter if she loved him—not if she couldn't trust him.

"It's good," she said finally.

Amanda's eyebrows rose. "Sure. I believe you. That only took a solid minute for you to say."

"Okay, here's the deal." She told her sister about Jack's proposition at the gala and then her reaction.

"Seriously? You had this chat *on* the dance floor in the middle of the gala and then you left him standing there alone?"

Serena scowled at her. "I didn't abandon him in the forest, Mandy. He's a grown man. I think he can find his own way off a dance floor."

"Not what I meant."

Serena didn't care what she meant. "I was proud of myself. Why aren't you?"

"Um, let's think. Since Jack's been back in your life, you've pulled off the event of the year and still managed to leave this damn building before eight o'clock every night. Alli's nuts about him and so are you, and you just tossed it all aside."

"I'm sorry." Serena stood up and glared down at her younger sister. "Yes, it's been fun since Jack's been back. I didn't expect to enjoy being with him, but I do. And, yes, before you ask, I do love him. But I'm not going to agree to less than I deserve because I love him. I'm also content with my life the way it is."

"Content?" Amanda shook her head. "That's pitiful. How many books and movies have you seen that brag about a *contented* ending?"

"This is real life, Amanda. Content should not be mocked." Drawing her head back, she almost stuck her tongue out at her. "Heck, you should be patting me on the back. He proposes without proposing and I said no. I took a stand."

"A stand against happiness. Bravo."

Irritated, Serena said, "You know what? I've changed a lot since Robert tossed a hand grenade into my life. And I'm glad to know that I can be good on my own."

"Notice you didn't say *happy*."

"I am happy. *Contentment* is actually a synonym for *happy*. And more than that, Alli's happy." She threw both hands up. "We have a terrific life together and I don't want anything to mess that up. Look, my career is going well. The family nonsense is quieting down—except for Bennett and Mom—and I have a gorgeous lover in my bed." Well, she had, until their talk at the gala. "I know

now that if Jack leaves again, I'll survive. I love him, yes. But not enough to risk Alli's heart—or my own, for that matter."

"What exactly are you risking?" Amanda asked quietly.

"Nothing," Serena argued. "That's the point."

"No," her sister told her quietly. "The point is, if you don't risk failure, you never really win."

"That makes no sense whatsoever."

Amanda laughed a little. "Sure it does. Think about it." Standing up, she said, "You have to be willing to put your heart on the line, Serena. Otherwise, you're just skimming the surface of a very deep pool and you'll never really be satisfied."

Her voice echoed in Serena's mind until she finally said, "Maybe not. But I'll be safe."

Amanda gave her a sad smile. "Is that really enough for you? Don't you deserve more?"

Jack should have been happy.

Hell, he was free again. There was no commitment holding him back. No one else to think of but himself. Why wasn't he *happy*, damn it? *Because*, a voice in his mind whispered, *being free doesn't mean a damn thing if all it buys you is emptiness*.

Sunlight drifted through the arched transom window over the front door and stretched out in long golden panels on the floor. He wandered through the empty halls of Colton house, and in his mind, he saw the ghosts of earlier generations walking these same floors. They'd lived and loved and built this place to last and it had.

What had he built, he wondered, beyond the bottom line of the Colton Group? Yes, he'd saved the company from his father's disastrous misman-agement, but he was still alone in a big house built for a family.

He stopped, turned around and stared down the long hall that stretched from the kitchen to the wide front doors.

The place was always immaculate and he had a housekeeper to thank for that. But then, there was never much to clean up, was there? There were no child-sized dirty footprints, no toys strewn across the floor. No slamming doors to shatter the quiet and no puppy running and skidding along the pol-ished wood planks.

He was a man alone, sitting on a mountain of success with no one to share it.

"Hell," he muttered, just to ease the quiet in the house, "I tried to share it, didn't I? Offered Serena and Alli a home here. She turned me down. What the hell else am I supposed to do?"

But then, that was a stupid question, wasn't it? He knew what he had to do, but he'd been too cow-ardly to do it. Like Serena had said, he hadn't of-fered to make any promises. He'd simply given her a chance for them to live together as separate entities in the same house. Like roommates with privileges. What was wrong with that?

"Damn it, she should be here. They should be here," he said aloud. He missed being with Serena. Laughing with her, talking about their days. He missed the sex, for sure, but not only that.

He missed the smell of her on his pillows. The casually tossed nightgown at the end of his bed. The sound of her in the shower and the squeal she made when he joined her.

Smiling to himself, he walked back down that long hallway, opened the front door and stepped outside. The sea air was cold and slapped at him, but he walked on. Around the house to the backyard that stood as a monument to a great gardener, but showed no signs of life beyond the well-tended plants and the expertly-trimmed grass and trees. Absently, he looked at a wide space of lawn and imagined a child-sized castle there with a blonde princess holding court.

Frowning, he shifted his gaze to beyond the retaining wall, where the ocean was loud and grumbling and the clouds gathered on the horizon looked as dangerous and angry as he felt.

A storm was coming and he would ride it out, alone with the echoes of other generations of Coltons. Instead of curling up on the couch with Alli and Serena and the puppy the little girl wanted so badly. He missed reading that tiny girl the books she loved so much. Missed hearing her laughter and the sly way she asked for what she wanted.

His backyard was empty, but it should have held Alli playing with her puppy while he and Serena watched from the flagstone patio.

And all of that might have happened if he'd been willing to take that final step. Risk it all on a roll of the dice.

He'd held back on making promises because of the damage he'd seen his father inflict on his mother. But, hell, his mom was happy now, in her second marriage. She had suffered the most, yet she was strong enough to take a chance. To put it all on the line and risk everything.

How could he do less?

The following day was Saturday and Serena had plans to spend every minute of it with Alli. Her talk with Amanda had made her think and she didn't like the answers she was coming up with. She had been devoting too much time to the company.

She'd wanted to make her own calls. Stand up for herself and take control of her life. Well, she'd proved she could do that, but what she had to do now was find balance. Her job. Her daughter. Her life. The most important of which was Alli.

They were going to the San Diego Zoo for the day and she wouldn't think about anything else but this precious time with her daughter. So when the knock on her front door sounded, she was more irritated than she might have been otherwise.

She opened it to find Jack standing there looking down at her and the expression on his face was unreadable.

"Well," she said, "I didn't expect to see you."

"I know." He slipped past her into the house as if half expecting her to shut the door in his face. "I need to talk to you. And Alli, too, but that's next. You're first."

She closed the door, turned around and leaned back against it while she watched him. "You'll have to make it fast. We're going to the zoo."

"Fine. I mean, good." Nodding, he pushed one hand through his hair and she took that split second to realize it looked as though he hadn't slept. For the first time since she'd known him, Jack looked...distracted. She had to wonder what was happening, and felt a flicker of worry for him.

God, she'd missed Jack. Her heartbeat thudded in her chest and love for the man swooped through her in a gigantic wave. Was Amanda right about him, too? About opening her heart, taking risks to get what she really wanted?

"Look," he said, splintering her thoughts, "what I said at the gala was stupid."

"Thanks," she said on a short laugh. What was she supposed to do with that? "I think."

"That came out wrong, too," he muttered and took a step toward her before stopping himself again. "You know, I never used to have trouble finding the right words. Hell, I *always* know what I'm doing, saying, thinking."

"Okay… Where are you going with this, Jack?"

"You're the reason my brain keeps tripping me up," he blurted out.

She had to laugh because he looked so frustrated. "Should I apologize?"

"No." Shaking his head, he pushed one hand through his hair and hurried on. "I went to the office yesterday to have this talk there, but I wanted Alli with us, too, and your company day care seems pretty fussy about who they turn children over to."

She smiled wryly. "I'll make sure they get a raise."

He nodded. Still distracted, he muttered, "The hell with it."

"What are you talking about, Jack?" she asked. "Or rather, what *aren't* you talking about? Why are you here?"

He walked to her, grabbed her shoulders and held on as if preventing her from escaping.

"Look, Serena, you deserve a hell of a lot more than me," he said. "I know that. So does Alli. But that's what I'm offering you both. Me."

Her heart actually stopped for one long moment

as she looked up into his dark blue eyes. Afraid to believe what she wanted to believe, Serena swallowed hard, held on to hope and asked, "What?"

He held on even tighter, and his thumbs rubbed her shoulders as if he needed the connection. Serena didn't know where he was going with all of this, but her heartbeat was racing. She couldn't take her eyes off him as he continued to speak.

"It's been a week since I've seen you and it's the longest week of my life. Damn it, Serena, I miss you. I miss Alli."

"We've missed you, too," she whispered, knowing it wasn't enough to describe what she and Alli had gone through over the last week. Countless times her daughter had asked her why Jack wasn't there. Or why couldn't they go see him. And Serena had felt the same way. It had taken every ounce of her self-control to keep from calling him. Seeing him.

"I want you back, Serena," he said tightly, his gaze burning into hers. "I know I said everything wrong at the gala. You had a right to be pissed and I don't blame you for walking away. But I'm here now and... Damn it, I wish I could find the pretty words you deserve, but all I can say is the plain truth. I want you in my life forever. I want to be Alli's dad and I'll try really hard not to screw that up."

Her heart simply flipped. Was this really happening? She lifted one hand to her mouth, but couldn't say a word. She didn't want to miss what he might say next. She hoped it would be more than the let's-play-house offer he'd made the last time. "What are you saying, Jack?"

"I'm saying I love you. And I love that little girl, too."

If her heart had flipped before, it was soaring now, making her a little light-headed. In the best possible way. A short choking sound shot from her throat. "I might need to sit down."

"No, you don't," he said, "because you've always known that I love you. I might have been too afraid to say it before, but it was still true."

"Oh, Jack…"

"I've always loved you. Always will. I want the three of us to be a family," Jack continued. "I want to marry you. Make more children with you and get Alli that puppy she wants. The castle, too."

"I don't believe this," she whispered, shaking her head, afraid that she might suddenly wake up from this lovely dream and find herself alone in bed. If that happened, her heart would literally break.

"Well, believe it," he urged. "The Colton house is big and empty, and it deserves to have laughter there again. It needs a family to bring it all the way back to life.

"And so do I."

He let her go long enough to dip into his pocket

and pull out a very familiar pale blue jeweler's box. Serena's breath caught in her chest as she realized what was actually happening. The one thing she'd wanted more than anything else in the world was opening up in front of her and she could hardly believe that a day trip to the zoo had been her planned highlight for the day.

He opened the box and a gorgeous emerald engagement ring sparkled up at her. "Oh, Jack…"

He took the ring from its velvet nest and held it out toward her. With his free hand, he tipped her chin up so he could look directly into her eyes. "I love you, Serena, and that's forever. That's what I'm asking you to give me. Forever. I walked away once and lost everything.

"Well, now I'm asking you to believe me and to trust me when I say I will never walk away again. I want to make a promise to you," he said, voice low and earnest, eyes burning into hers. "To Alli. I want that commitment, Serena. I want the future we can build together."

"I can't believe you're saying all of this," she said, looking for the reassurance she needed in the depths of his eyes. When she saw it, the truth nearly buckled her knees.

"Believe it," he said firmly. "Believe *me*. Believe *this*."

He bent his head, kissed her and then looked into her eyes again. "Trust me, Serena. Trust me with your heart and trust me with Alli's. I will never let either of you down."

As if he'd conjured her by saying her name, the little girl ran into the room and skidded to a stop when she spotted him. "Jack! You're here! Are you going to the zoo with us? We're gonna see monkeys and tigers and bears…"

He grinned, picked her up and hooked the tiny blonde on his left arm while he held the emerald ring out to Serena in his right hand. "There's nothing I want more than to be with you two, and I would love to go to the zoo with you," he said, then shifted his gaze to Serena. "Let's ask your mom if I can be with you guys. At the zoo."

"Mommy, *please*." Alli hooked one arm around Jack's neck and leaned into him.

Staying with the zoo analogy, Serena looked from her daughter to the man she loved with all of her heart. In his eyes, she saw everything she'd ever wanted shining back at her. All she had to do was stand up for herself and take what she wanted. Make the decision that would bring them all together. That would create the kind of happiness she'd always dreamed of.

As Amanda had said, if you risked nothing, you never really won.

Heart full, she said, "If we go to the zoo together, I'll still want to keep working at the company…"

"Not a problem. I love my job, too, but we can

still go to the zoo." He shrugged. "Sometimes I'd have to go to the zoo in Europe, but you and Alli can go with me."

"What's Europe?" Alli asked. "And when do we go to the zoo?"

Serena rose up, kissed her daughter's cheek, then kissed Jack. Alli laughed in delight. "The zoo with you sounds perfect," Serena said finally and held out her left hand.

Jack slid the ring onto her finger and Alli said, "Ooh, pretty."

Jack smiled at her. "You're prettier."

She cupped his face in her small hands. "Can we go to the zoo now?"

"Yes, we can," Serena said, stepping into the circle of Jack's right arm. "All three of us. Together."

Jack folded his girls close and held on tightly. Then he looked at Alli and said, "How would you like to come live at my house?"

She looked at her mother first, then smiled at Jack. "For always?"

He glanced at Serena, then promised her daughter, "Always."

"With a castle? And a puppy?"

Serena laughed and Jack grinned down at her. "She's a tough negotiator."

"You have no idea," Serena said, laughing.

"I'll learn," he assured her with a wide grin.

"How about," Jack said, "you get a castle and a puppy and a new daddy?"

Alli's mouth dropped open and her eyes went wide and astonished. "*You* would be my daddy? For really?"

"For really," Serena said, looking up at Jack. The happiness on her daughter's face echoed the joy in Serena's heart and she knew this was the best decision she'd ever made in her life.

"This is the best day!" Alli crowed, hugged Jack and then asked, "Can we go to the zoo now, Daddy?"

"You bet we can," Jack said, and his voice thickened with the same emotions choking Serena.

"I love you," she whispered.

"I love you more," he assured her, and, in that moment, the three of them became the family they were meant to be.

* * * * *

Look for Bennett's story,
The Wrong Mr. Right
Available next month!

COMING NEXT MONTH FROM

HARLEQUIN
DESIRE

#2839 WHAT HE WANTS FOR CHRISTMAS
Westmoreland Legacy: The Outlaws • by Brenda Jackson
After a decade apart, COO Sloan Outlaw isn't looking to get back with ex Lesley Cassidy. But with her company facing a hostile takeover, he offers his assistance...if she joins him at his luxury cabin. But when they find themselves snowed in, the heat ignites...

#2840 HOW TO HANDLE A HEARTBREAKER
Texas Cattleman's Club: Fathers and Sons • by Joss Wood
Gaining independence from her wealthy family, officer and law student Hayley Lopez is rarely intimidated, especially by the likes of billionaire playboy developer Jackson Michaels. An advocate for the underdog, Hayley clashes often with Jackson. But will one hot night together change everything?

#2841 THE WRONG MR. RIGHT
Dynasties: The Carey Center • by Maureen Child
For contractor Hannah Yates, the offer to work on CEO Bennett Carey's project is a boon. Hired to repair his luxury namesake restaurant, she finds his constant presence and good looks...distracting. Burned before, she won't lose focus, but the sparks between them can't be ignored...

#2842 HOLIDAY PLAYBOOK
Locketts of Tuxedo Park • by Yahrah St. John
Advertising exec Giana Lockett has a lot to prove to her football dynasty family, and landing sports drink CEO Wynn Starks's account is crucial. But their undeniable attraction is an unforeseen complication. Will they be able to make the winning play to save their relationship and business deal?

#2843 INCONVENIENT ATTRACTION
The Eddington Heirs • by Zuri Day
When wealthy businessman Cayden Barker is blindsided by Avery Gray, it's not just by her beauty—her car accidently hits his. And then they meet again unexpectedly—at the country club where he's a member and she's employed. Is this off-limits match meant to last?

#2844 BACKSTAGE BENEFITS
Devereaux Inc. • by LaQuette
TV producer Josiah Manning needs to secure lifestyle guru Lyric Smith as host of his new show. As tempting as the offer—and producer—is, Lyric is hesitant. But as a rival emerges, will they take the stage together or let the curtain fall on their sizzling chemistry?

YOU CAN FIND MORE INFORMATION ON UPCOMING HARLEQUIN TITLES, FREE EXCERPTS AND MORE AT HARLEQUIN.COM.

HDCNM1121

"What do you want to ask me, Sloan?"

He drew in a deep breath. "I need to know what made you
come looking for me last night."

She broke eye contact with him and glanced out the
window, not saying anything for a moment. "You were gone
longer than you said you would be. I got worried. It was either
go see what was taking you so long or pace the floor with
worry even more. I chose the former."

"But the weather had turned into a blizzard, Les." He then
realized he'd called her what he'd normally called her while
they'd been together. She had been Les and not Leslie.

"I know that. I also knew you were out there in it. I tried
to convince myself that you could take care of yourself, but I
also knew with the amount of wind blowing and snow coming
down that anything could have happened."

She paused again before saying, "Chances are, you would
have made it back to the cabin, but I couldn't risk the chance
you would not have."

He tried not to concentrate on the sadness he heard in her
voice and saw in her eyes. Instead, he concentrated on her

mouth and in doing so was reminded of just how it tasted. "Not sure if I would have made it back, Les. My head was hurting, and it was getting harder and harder to make my body move because I was so cold. Hell, I wasn't even sure I was going in the right direction. I regret you put your own life at risk, but I'm damn glad you were there when I needed you."

"Just like you were there for me and my company when I needed you, Sloan," she said softly.

Her words made him realize that they'd been there for each other when it had mattered the most. He didn't want to think what would have been the outcome if he'd been at the cabin alone as originally planned and the snowstorm hit. Nor did he want to think what would have happened to her and her company if Redford hadn't told him what was going on. The potential outcome of either made him shiver.

"You're still cold. I'd better go and get that hot chocolate going," she said, shifting to get up and reach for her clothes.

"Don't go yet," he said, not ready for any distance to be put between them or their bodies.

She glanced over at him. Their gazes held and then, as if she'd just noticed his erection pressing against her thigh, she said, "You do know the only reason why we're naked in this sleeping bag together, right?"

He nodded. "Yes. Because I needed your body's heat last night." He inched his mouth closer to hers and then said, "Only problem is, I still need your body's heat, Les. But now I need it for a totally different reason."

And then he leaned in and kissed her.

Don't miss what happens next in...
What He Wants for Christmas *by Brenda Jackson,*
the next book in her Westmoreland Legacy:
The Outlaws series!

Available December 2021 wherever
Harlequin Desire books and ebooks are sold.

Harlequin.com